Jackman's Cliff

Tales to take you Beyond the Brink

Cliff Jackman

Manor House

Library and Archives Canada
Cataloguing in Publication

Jackman, Cliff, 1980-, author
        Jackman's cliff : tales to take you beyond the brink
/ Cliff Jackman.

  ISBN 978-1-897453-39-1 (pbk.)

        I. Title.

PS8619.A224J33 2013   C813'.6   C2013-906046-4

Printed and bound in Canada
First Edition.
144 pages.
All rights reserved.

Cover design: Donovan Davie and Michael B. Davie
Cover art by Shutterstock

Published October 15, 2013
Manor House Publishing Inc.
www.manor-house.biz
(905) 648-2193

We gratefully acknowledge the financial support of the Government of
Canada through Book Fund Canada, Dept. of Canadian Heritage.

Manor House Publishing Inc.
www.manor-house.biz
905-648-2193

1 Father's Day

My heart leaps up when I behold
  A rainbow in the sky:
So was it when my life began;
So is it now I am a man;
So be it when I shall grow old,
  Or let me die!
The Child is father of the Man;
  I could wish my days to be
Bound each to each by natural piety.

William Wordsworth

Father's Day is celebrated the third Sunday of June and my father, Charlie Livingstone, was born on the 17th of June, and so occasionally his birthday and Father's Day coincided. In such years he used to complain, or to pretend to complain, that he was getting cheated of one of his "Dad Days." It was like having your birthday on Christmas, he used to say. You got screwed out of half your gifts.

As you may or may not recall, Father's Day fell on June 17th in 2052. My father was born in 1982, and so, well, you can do the math for yourself I guess. He didn't make too many jokes about losing a "Dad Day" that year. Just one, as we were walking out of one of the god-awful group therapy sessions they make you go to, you know, with the plastic chairs and the terrible fake coffee in the big dispensers and the peanut butter cookies with the machine-made fork-marks on top. And it wasn't much of a joke, either; he just looked at me and smiled wryly and said: "Worst birthday ever. Worst Father's Day ever. What a rip-off."

I smiled at him; I'd been a little surprised how well he'd taken everything. We'd gone through the same thing with Mom two years before. She'd taken it like a pro, of course. I think being able to prepare for the end really suited her. She was a strong person and she met death like she met everything, head-on, with no excuses or regrets.

Dad was different. He was a big guy, taller with broad shoulders, but he was terribly anxious and he had worried about hurting people's feelings his whole life. He was a bit of a dreamer and he was always forgetting things, important things. Mom always used to flip out on him. She was short and thin and beautiful and I'd always wondered how they got together. I finally asked Dad about it at her funeral.

"Simple," he'd said. "Your mother was 31 and she was looking for a man but she wasn't having any luck because she was hell to get along with and she was working till midnight every night. So one day, I walk into her office. I'm two years behind her at McCarthy's and I'm about to get fired, because I hate it there and my work is sloppy. I'm tall and handsome and I'm easy to get along with. I'm actually scared to death of her because she makes me work all the time. And she looks at me and she thinks: why not? And then you came around two years later."

"Thanks for that Dad," I'd replied.

Anyway, like I said, I was kind of surprised how good he was about everything. But the thing about my Dad, he was a bit lazy, and he was a bit of a goof, but he was as smart as fuck. You had to give it to the old man. Smarter than me, smarter than Janie, even smarter than Mom, really. And so when we went to pick him up Sunday morning, Father's Day morning, he was gone.

"He was taking it so well," Chelsea said, surprised, as we poked around the house.

"Yeah, well, that's Dad," I said.

Once we'd satisfied ourselves he'd flown the coop we took the metro to the Euthanos Centre. We went in the front door and I walked over those slick tiles, you know the tiles they have, glossy, almost, and I was came up to the main desk and all I had to say was: "It's my dad, Charlie Livingtsone's, seventieth birthday, and I went to his house to bring him here, but he wasn't there." No biggie, no shame in that, happens all the time, who can really blame the old bugger. Etc. And then I could just go home and keep breathing till 2081 or earlier.

But when I got there, I couldn't do it. I stood there. I knew I had to do it, and I knew there was no use in not doing it. They were expecting him and when he didn't show up, they'd know. But I couldn't do it. I just stood there, impotent and helpless, thinking of Dad.

Chelsea looked at me and, God bless her, she walked over and did it for me. Then we walked back out and she didn't mention a thing.

The cops searched the house the day after Father's Day, the Monday. I was at work. When I got home Luke was crying. Luke's my three-year-old son. Apparently the cops had been asking him questions and he was scared and confused. It was in his head that Grandpa was out somewhere and people were looking for him and we had to go find him, we had to go help him.

Apparently the cop had been pretty ashamed. He said to Chelsea that we were lucky to have him. I guess he might not have had much experience with kids. We'd tried everything to have Luke; my parents had put up a lot of cash on every test-tube fertility gizmo you could think of. Then we gave up and he came two years later, when Chelsea was thirty seven. Our miracle baby. We loaned him out on weekends to Chelsea's childless friends and his crude, vibrant finger-paintings hung on the walls in my coworkers' offices.

We had a house we'd bought with the inheritance. Nothing too fancy, just a little three bedroom place in Etobicoke about a five minute walk from the lake. One of the new and efficient semi-detached bungalows they'd built after the war. Every night Chelsea and I would sit together in our family room and watch the news after Luke had gone to bed. This I could have done without, it was depressing, but Chelsea insisted on it. I thought she somehow implied that it was our duty, although we were obviously powerless to do anything about the things we saw.

The day my father arrived at our house the lead story was famine and threats from China, as usual. Natural disasters came second, and then war. But the last news items were, to me, always the worst: terrible things that no one could explain. All the hummingbirds would be dying, for instance, or a particular kind of plankton. Fish populations not recovering, even if they should. Unusually high levels of mercury in dairy products. The bad things we had coming to us, I figured, were bad enough. How much worse, then, these horrible mysteries.

Just as Chelsea and I were preparing to head up for bed, there was Dad, climbing over our back fence. Chelsea saw him and said: "Oh God." The tone of her voice was hard to describe. Not frustrated or angry or afraid. Just a little apprehensive. Like: here we go.

I opened the sliding glass door.

"Dad," I said. "What are you doing?"

He looked abashed. I guess you get the idea I never had an overpowering authority figure type father. But still, it was weird to see him looking down at his shoes, embarrassed, like he was ashamed of something in front of me, his son. I felt odd.

"Where have you been?" I said.

"Can I come in?" Dad said.

"Sure."

He wiped his shoes, then thought, then just took them off and slid the door closed behind him.

"Hi Charlie," Chelsea said.

"Hi Chelsea," Charlie said.

He stood, uncertain for a moment, then sat down in a small chair. His spindly knees came almost to his chin.

I was still standing; after a moment, I sat back down on the couch next to Chelsea.

"Dad. What are you doing?"

"Nothing."

"This just makes things harder for us."

"I know. It's selfish of me."

"You could get us into trouble."

"I know."

"If I hide you here ..."

"I need a favour," Dad said. "I need you to drive me to Deep River."

"Pardon?"

Dad smiled a little. He'd been paunchy in his fifties and sixties, but he'd lost a lot since Mom died. Now he was gaunt, almost skeletal.

"You remember Robby Mercer? Your mom's ex-partner?"

"You want to go to Robby Mercer's cottage?"

"He left it to a trust for his kids. But they don't go there anymore. Two of them are dead, the third is overseas. The place is isolated and it's really set-up. I've been putting canned goods there all year, and it has a good garden. I could hide a long time."

"What are you talking about?" I said.

"I'm sorry, I wasn't going to ask you. My ride fell through."

"You'd be like a prisoner Dad. What's the point?"

Elderly people develop a little smile, kind of sad and tolerant, and they save it for when they recognized their failings in the younger generation. Dad smiled this smile at me now.

"Keep living son, that's all."

"Oh fuck," I said, and put my hand over my mouth.

"No," Chelsea said.

She smiled.

"You don't have to," Dad said.

"Well, the answer is no. I'm sorry Charlie. I truly am. I went through this with my father, I'll have to do it with my mother some day. We are not going to risk losing everything for this. You have to go sometime. It's natural."

"I'm asking Charlie, Chelsea," Dad said.

"You can't just go around me," Chelsea said. "He can't just make this decision without me."

"I can do what I want, Chelsea," I said.

"No you can't!" she said. "Charlie, do you want a drink before I call the police?"

For some reason I was getting angry. I would never even have said I was that close to Dad, although I loved him, of course. But Chelsea's attitude was a little much. So I laid the hammer down.

"You call the police," I said, "and I'll put dad in the car and start driving."

Her mouth set in a thin line.

"You can't do this to me. You can't just do this on your own."

"He's my dad," I said. "It's my decision."

"No, it's our decision."

"What does that mean, 'our' decision? That I have to do what you say? We can't take a vote. There's only two of us!"

Dad went into the kitchen.

"He's seventy," she said. "He's already lived his life. And now you're going to risk everything to drive him up to a cottage? For him to hide in a cottage? For how long? Six months? A year? Of living in exile? What's the point of that? What are you really gaining?"

"He's my dad."

"What do you mean, he's your dad? Sure he's your dad. Everyone loses their dad sooner or later. It's the law! Okay? It's the law. You will lose your job, you will go to jail, we will lose the house, Luke will grow up without his dad," and now she started to tear up, "and for what? He's had his life. He's had a good life."

I didn't say anything; I just shut off the video. The screen hissed back up into the ceiling, revealing a laminated poster of a Picasso painting.

"And you know what?" Chelsea sobbed. "It's their fault. I'm sorry. It's their fault. We didn't mess up the planet. We didn't raise the ocean levels. We didn't burn the hole in the ozone layer and fill up the atmosphere with garbage and ... use up all the oil and spread nuclear waste around. That was them! That was them and their ... their two-car garage lifestyle. It's their fault there isn't enough food. It's their fault there isn't enough electricity. It's their fault people can't afford houses and live in shitty slums. There's nine billion people on earth and twice as many of them are over sixty-five as under eighteen. We can't afford to keep them. They aren't useful and they've led good lives and it doesn't hurt them at all. It doesn't hurt at all."

Her voice had gotten rather loud and upstairs Luke started to cry. Chelsea and I looked at each other. She didn't move. I went upstairs.

I turned on the light. Luke looked at me.

"Shh shh shh," I said.

"Daddy!" he said.

I picked him up and cradled him in my arms. He was so small and helpless and life was hard, so hard, and the world was so fucked up. I felt a powerful urge to cry. I rarely cried. My Dad was a bit of a crier, he'd get so wound up over something he'd let out these little sobs. Not me. I didn't cry. Especially not in front of my son.

"Where's Grandpa?" he said. "I want to see Grandpa."

"He's gone away on a trip."

"When's he coming back?"

"I don't know. Soon."

"When will I be able to see Grandpa?"

"Soon," I said, "soon."

I wondered if the world would be a better place if we could bear to tell the truth to our children and I decided it would not. I also decided that after work tomorrow I would drive my father to this fucking cottage in Deep River.

Oh, I knew the law was a very good law; to know that you only had to remember how much we had been spending on social security and health care for the last year of life. All you had to do was to remember the failed crops and the dirty air and the dying hummingbirds and the fucking fish that stubbornly refused to come back. Yes, the law was a very good law when it concerned other people's fathers, it was profoundly sensible, and I thought I had been ready to let them kill him, but I knew in my heart of hearts that although I could kill my father I could not kill my sister's father, mother's husband, and especially not my son's grandfather. That was how they got you.

I walked downstairs ready to explain this to Chelsea, still holding back tears a little, when I saw her speaking with my father in the kitchen. Dad looked at me and then he looked back at Chelsea and he winked and smiled and patted his pocket. She looked at him and then she turned and looked at me and then she brushed past me to walk upstairs.

"I straightened it out," he said. "Don't worry."

"How did you do that?"

"Twenty-five years of legal experience. Negotiation, my boy. Getting to yes."

"Where am I even going to get a car?" I said.

"I have a car," Dad said. "I just didn't have a driver."

He gave me an address.

"Thought of everything, huh?" I asked.

"I guess so."

"I'll try to get out early tomorrow," I said. "Stay in the basement. For God's sake, don't let Luke see you."

"I wouldn't want to upset him. I think your boy saved my bacon anyway. We heard him down here."

"Yeah," I said. "Lucky for you."

I gave him a hug. He went down into the basement and I went up and lay next to my wife. I thought she'd be pretty pissed at me, but when I got under the sheets she turned around and pressed up against me with an intensity that took me by surprise.

After a stressful day at work I took the train up to the address Dad gave me. The car had a full charge. More than enough to get to Deep River and back. I waited until quite late, after midnight, and then I drove into Etobicoke. When I got to my street I turned the lights off. The engine was completely silent. My dad came out of the house and got in the trunk. Then I stepped on the accelerator and got back on the highway.

I was sweating it until we got out of the city, but then I felt much better. I hadn't driven since we took a trip to Montreal before Luke was born, but it wasn't hard with no traffic. Just blowing by the big trucks, one after another. Once we got off the 401 I got a little anxious about my poor tall father and I pulled over at a closed-up gas station, parking out back towards the trees.

I opened the trunk and gave Dad a bottle of water. He was happy.

"How far are we?"

"We just turned on to the 115."

"What a trip," he said. "Father and son."

"You can piss in the bottle when you finish it," I said.

"You've thought of everything," he said. "Did I ever tell you how proud of you I am?"

"Yeah," I said.

"Well, it's true. I'm so proud of you and everything you've done. You know the thing with kids? You can't do everything for them that you want to. You can feed them, clothe them, teach them. But you can't make them friends, you can't help them fall in love, you can't help them pick a career. They have to do all that on their own. And it's so hard, so very hard. Just because most people do it doesn't mean it's not hard. I remember when I came home one day and you were crying. You must have been fourteen."

I was a little taken aback; I remembered now but I'd forgotten.

"And I said what's wrong? And you wouldn't tell me. I think you were just depressed. And I felt so powerless. I just wanted for you to be happy. But what could I do? I could just say I loved you. But so what, right? Everyone's Dad loves them. There's nothing I could do. But you grew up so well. I couldn't believe I did it. I failed at everything I ever did except you, kid. You're the best thing."

"What about Janie?"

"Janie."

She'd died in a terrorist attack ten years ago. I suddenly felt awkward for having brought her up.

"Good driving son," Dad said. "Don't make any sudden turns or anything.

It was two in the morning and I closed the trunk.

We got to Deep River before the sunrise. The road to the cottage was one of those long, windy one-lane cottage roads that goes up and down hills and where you have to navigate by looking at little hand-made signs nailed to trees. I thought about getting Dad up to help, especially since it must be getting bumpy back there, but we were too close, way too close, for anything like that. I was just going to drop him off, turn around, drive home, and plead the Fifth if this ever came up again. And I'd always be able to look my son in the eye.

The cottage was at the very end of the road, a full mile past any of the others. Mercer had bought up the land when it was cheap. Afterwards it had gotten expensive. Now, of course, it was worthless; there were no more jet-skis, air-conditioned second homes with satellite TVs, or weekend warriors. Those days were gone.

I finally pulled the car up onto the yellowing lawn next to the small cottage, crouched up against the lake like an animal taking a drink. I stepped outside and opened the trunk. Dad groaned as I helped him out; I heard his back crack audibly.

"We did it," he said.

"You did it, anyway," I said. "I still have to get back to the city."

"You'll be fine," he said. "Leave the car where I told you. It'll be gone Sunday morning. No one will be the wiser."

We walked up to the front door and fumbled with the key in the lock when we the light splashed over us. The car had been running with its lights off and hadn't made a sound. We turned around.

It was a police cruiser.

"Stay calm," Dad said.

My mouth was dry. My stomach felt like it was filling with air.

A cop got out. Young fellow, with blonde sideburns. The headlights went out and everything was dark.

"Who are you?" he said.

"My name's Brad Mercer," Dad said. "What are you doing on my property?"

The flashlight clicked on and shone on us. I squinted and held out my hand; Dad never moved.

"We've had break-ins," the cop said. "Can I see some identification?"

"You can't come onto my property, private property, and ask me to show identification," Dad said.

"I'd still like to see some ID," the cop said.

Dad said again that there was no law saying you had to give the cops your ID. This, of course, was correct. However, there was also no good reason not to show a cop your ID unless you were a crook.

"Sir," the cop said finally, "I don't care if you are a lawyer, show me some goddamn ID."

Poor Dad. He had gotten so close. But he'd never been that close, I guess, not really.

"You want to see my ID?" Dad said, his old man's voice going high and whiny, and that's when he pulled the gun.

"Holy shit!" I screamed.

Dad fired once, well above the cop's head. The cop drew like Clint Eastwood and shot my father three times, centre mass. It still ended up taking him an awful long time to die. The cop was with him when he passed; I was cuffed in the cruiser. At one point my dad lifted one bloody fist and gave me a thumbs-up and that's when I started to cry.

What saved me in the end was being a lawyer's child. I didn't say anything. Not in the car, not in the police station, not in the Don Jail, where I was quickly separated from my jacket, pants and shoes by the other prisoners.

They brought me into an interrogation room after I'd been in jail for two days. There were two cops. One of them was older with thinning white hair. He didn't seem concerned. The other was some bureaucratic true believer, younger and mean-looking, and he was pissed.

"Can I ask you something?" the young cop said.

"Yeah," I said, "but I'm not going to answer."

"The officer who apprehended you said you looked pretty surprised to see the gun. When the gun came out? That right? You surprised to see the gun?"

I said nothing.

"You didn't know he had a gun, right?"

Silence.

"Fuck you. Let me ask you one more goddamn thing. How'd your father compel you to drive him up to this cottage from the trunk?"

More silence, now I was smiling a little. Sad and tolerant. Getting older after all.

They let me out a few hours later. No charges. My wife had told them that Dad had threatened to kill me. They knew it was bullshit; I'd sat in jail for two days without mentioning that I'd been threatened. But they had no proof. You can't hold someone's silence against them in court. You can't even mention it. So they had nothing to go on.

My wife kissed me very hard when I walked in the front door and then we had lunch. Luke was over at one of my wife's friends houses on loan. We made love and then we lay next to each other for a while. She was kind of tracing her fingers down my side. It felt nice. For a while I couldn't help thinking of 2081, when my number would come up. But I am not a morbid man, and those thoughts passed.

"Charlie thought I let you go because he showed me the gun," Chelsea said. "But it was because of Luke."

"He knew it was because of Luke," I said.

We got the little man back in time for dinner and I tucked him into bed that night.

"Did you see Grandpa on your trip?" he asked.

"Yes, I did," I said. "He misses you very much."

"When's he coming home?"

"Not for a while. It's a very long trip."

"But I'll see him when he gets back?"

"Oh yes," I said. "You'll see him when he comes back. Grandpa wouldn't miss a chance to see you, if he got one."

2 Haunted

1. inhabited or frequented by ghosts.
2. preoccupied, as with an emotion, memory, or idea; obsessed.
3. disturbed; distressed; worried.

Northumberland County is made up of some pretty country: gently rolling hills, forests of old trees, hayfields separated by split-rail fences. Neal liked it the first time he came into it, driving up a smooth dirt road that didn't go more than fifty feet without turning a corner.

He also liked the first house the real estate agent took them to look at. It was about halfway between Cobourg and Rice Lake, on the top of a hill, and it was built according to someone's idea in 1969 of what would be fashionable in 2011. Lots of wood panelling, shag carpeting, fluorescent lighting, and big picture windows from which you could see almost all the way to Lake Ontario.

But most of all, Neal liked the barn. The Realtor had warned them it was a little run down, and it was, but it wasn't a desiccated old shack. It was about six hundred square feet and made of big heavy beams. Neal could tell it would be a great place to record. The sound would just be like an old church.

LaTanya was a bit put off by the carpeting and some other cosmetic issues with the inside of the house which Neal considered to be pure chickenshit, especially since he would be the one fixing the place up. She made him go see a couple of other places, but she gave in eventually.

The whole property was fifteen acres and it wasn't cheap. LaTanya made a good salary as a nurse, especially when you figured that she didn't have to worry about retirement, and Neal always made more money than you might expect, between royalties and other odds and sods, but they never could have come close to affording it if they hadn't been able to sell their old house in the Beaches for a truly astonishing sum. Neal was so grateful to the idiot yuppies that won the protracted bidding war that he patiently talked to them about music for at least fifteen minutes, even though it made his back teeth hurt to do it.

The place did not have the reputation of being haunted, and the Realtor did not mention a ghost.

They moved in July 1st to make it easier for the kids. Neal spent most of the summer working on the house. It only took a couple of weeks to rip out the carpet and put down some laminate. That made LaTanya felt much better. Next he painted, put up some wallpaper, and changed the light fixtures. They agreed to delay doing the kitchens and the bathrooms till next year, so he could save his time and their money for the recording studio in the barn.

After the kids were settled in school he spent most of the fall working on the barn. Those were some good days. He'd get up when LaTanya and the kids were leaving. Once everyone was out the door he'd turn the fucking TV off, drink coffee from his French press, read *The Economist* on their back porch and look at the view and the birds pecking at the feeder and the squirrels scampering around.

Then he'd play the guitar in the barn, listening to the sound bounce off those walls, singing one love song after another in his halting, earnest voice. He would work for a few hours, putting up the panelling on the walls and doing the wiring. After lunch he'd get some exercise, lifting weights inside if the weather was bad, biking or running on the old country roads if it was fine. By the time he showered it was almost time for the kids to come back.

There were not many signs the barn was haunted. A few things would go missing and turn up in strange places. Others would fall off the work bench when they hadn't been anywhere near the edge. The door swung open and closed when there was no wind. One time Neal heard a sound like crying outside. It was loud enough for him to stop what he was doing, wipe the stinging sweat out of his eyes, and listen, but then it went away and he assumed he'd imagined it.

One morning in mid-October it got so cold that Neal could see his breath. When Neal turned off his tablesaw and went outside it was fifteen degrees outside and sunny, but the skin of his arms was still stiff with the cold and covered in goosebumps. The temperature went back to normal inside, but he was still a bit unsettled and he felt like he was being watched. He gave up working for the day and went inside and made himself a virgin Caesar.

He did not actually see the ghost until the winter.

There was a lot of snow that winter, which was fine with Neal. He liked to shovel the path between the sliding glass door at the back of their house and the studio. Although he wasn't doing much recording, and he hadn't yet started renting the place out (he was saving that for spring), he religiously shovelled that path after every snowfall.

One evening they attended a neighbourhood Christmas party and returned home late. LaTanya curled up in the corner of their leather couch and turned on the television to watch something dreadful, *Say Yes to the Dress* or *Storage Wars* or some shit like that. That was Neal's signal to do some shovelling; never mind that it would probably snow again before morning.

He was working up a good sweat when he heard the sound. Like a ringing in his ears, but curiously living. A keening noise. Like a mouse in pain, or an oyster singing.

He looked up and saw her standing next to the barn. It never occurred to him for a moment that she was anything other than a ghost. She was walking on top of the snow without breaking through, but it was still more than that. It was how dark she was. How elastic her edges. How quickly she moved towards him, and how smoothly, as if she was standing on a conveyer belt. How wrong she was, in general.

"Oh god!" Neal said, his voice, weirdly high and weak.

The ghost's eyes were black marbles, like the eyes of a shark.

Neal fell down backwards in the snow and rolled over and sprinted to the back door. He didn't dare to look behind him. It felt as if his heart had stopped in his chest. For a moment his frozen fingers fumbled with the handle but then the door slid open and he stumbled into the mudroom and slammed the door shut behind him.

"Neal?" LaTanya called. "Neal?"

He heard her feet on the stairs as she came up from the basement. When she arrived Neal was bent over, leaning on his knees, panting for air.

"Neal, you scared the life out of me! Are you all right?"

LaTanya was tall and black, with long braided hair interwoven with beads. She had been very beautiful, once upon a time, but she had always inclined to puffiness. After the birth of her second child she became heavy, despite that she was a reasonably light eater and ran five miles three times a week. Neal, on the other hand, with little to do during his days other than work out, was fitter and leaner than ever, with muscular arms and a narrow waist.

He looked at his wife and tried to speak, but he didn't quite manage it.

LaTanya's pretty eyes widened.

"You look like you've seen a ghost!" she said.

Neal lay in bed that night with one of his wife's warm, slightly meaty arms lying across his chest. He stared at the ceiling. He couldn't get the image of the ghost out of his mind. The more he pictured her in his mind, the more her beauty haunted him. The perfect lines of her body. Alien and insubstantial, but glowing and soft. Knowing that he couldn't touch her, that his hand would pass right through her, somehow only inflamed his desire to try. How queer it was to be haunted with desire for something you knew was so useless.

For the next few days he didn't go back to the barn. He had plenty of excuses not to; the kids were out of school and his wife was on hollday. They spent a lot of time cross-country skiing around the property, forging trails through the leaf-less trees and finding hidden mysteries: old broken-down fences, cow skulls perched on branches, rusted bits of machinery that seemed relics of a by-gone age.

The afternoon of December 23rd Neal was making eggnog. LaTanya would have been happy enough to buy it at the store, but Neal was very fastidious about food and he had plenty of time on his hands, so he liked to make everything himself; bread, pasta, salsa, hummus. Now eggnog. He was just sprinkling the nutmeg in each mug when the phone began to ring. There followed the stomping of Nancy's feet on the floor, and then she shouted: "Dad! Phone!"

Neal picked up the phone.

"Hey buddy," Blake said. "Merry Christmas."

Neal felt an uncomfortable sensation in his stomach, like a snake slithering around.

"Hey man. Merry Christmas to you too."

After the band had broken up, they had not spoken for five years. Blake had called him out of the blue six months ago. The call had been anticlimactic, for the simple reason that it had not felt like it had been very long since they had spoken. It wasn't that the time had passed quickly, although it had. It was that Neal felt as if they had never really been apart. Because every time he had seen something or heard something or done something he had always known what Blake would have thought and said about that thing. They had spent so much time together, and been so incredibly close, that there was nothing they could do to surprise each other any longer. Five minutes after their conversation, he hadn't been able to tell LaTanya what they'd talked about.

"How's the family doing?" Blake asked.

"Good," Neal said.

"What are you getting Sid?"

"PSP."

"What?"

"PSP. Playstation Portable."

"Oh."

"Against my better instincts, really."

"You should get him an iPad."

"They're overpriced."

"I've got an iPad," Blake said. "I take it on tour with me. It's great. I find so many ways to use it."

"We have a netbook," Neal said.

"What about Nancy?"

"Riding stuff. Breeches, helmet. We're going to put her in riding lessons."

"Horseback riding?"

"Yes."

"Wow, great."

"How are you? Still in Florida?"

"Yeah," Blake laughed, sounding breezy and confident. "Just another day in paradise man! What can I say? I'm looking at palm trees now."

"Wow."

"I'm on a boat, actually."

Neal suppressed a snicker.

For a moment Blake was quiet, a bit startled. Offended.

"You just reminded me of that Saturday Night Live song," Neal said. "That's all."

"Oh!" Blake said, and then laughed his hearty, I'm-so-confident laugh again.

"Anyway," Neal said. "Sounds like you're living the life. How's the rest of the band?"

"Well, Jhonny's good," Blake said. "I talked to him yesterday. But Alistair, not so much. I fired him."

"Really?"

"Yeah man. He was coasting. And I just don't have any tolerance for that shit. You know me. Oars in the water. Everyone's got to be giving 110%."

"It's your band," Neal said.

"Anyway, that's the reason I'm calling you."

The snake bit something in his abdomen. The venom felt like ice.

"What?" Neal said.

"I've got a big tour lined up this year, plus Lolapalooza," Blake said. "And I need a bassist. What do you say?"

"Oh man," Neal said. "No, no, man."

"What? What the fuck are you talking about?"

"No, no," Neal said. "I'm retired man."

"Yeah I get it. But we're not talking about you rejoining the band. We're just talking about one tour. For old time's sake."

"Dude, no. I don't even play bass."

"Okay, fuck that. Yes you do. You fucking play everything. Don't you think I know that?"

"I'm retired."

"Exactly, you're retired," Blake said. "Exactly. So I know you aren't doing anything next summer."

"Look," Neal said. "I'm just done with touring and that stuff, okay? I just don't want to do it."

"Why are you so fucking bitter about this?" Blake said, a little anger creeping into his voice.

"I'm not bitter," Neal said. He was getting angry too, he couldn't help it.

"Yes you are," Blake said. "It fucking kills you that I made it big. It eats you up inside."

Neal held the phone away from his mouth. He visualized himself saying: *And it kills you to hear people, even if it's only a few snotty hipsters, say that your best albums were when I was in your band (no, when I was running your band; even though you told the chicks "we don't really have a LEAD guitarist, we take it song by song.") Even with all your money and your fame and your bimbos and your marlin fishing in December, even with all that, it kills you when you go on Pitchfork to read what people are saying about you (like you always do, you vain son of a bitch) and you see that some nobody college student is calling you a sell out. Because nothing is ever enough for you, you lunatic. And that's why I don't want to go on your tour.*

As he thought these thoughts, Neal saw, through the kitchen window, a doe bound through the back yard. Leaving tiny neat tracks behind it. It went into the trees next to the barn and it was gone.

"Look," Neal said. "You want to hang out. Fine. Good. Come up here. I'm going to build a barbeque pit in the spring. I've got a studio."

"Oh yeah, I heard about that," Blake said, his voice dripping with what would sound to an outsider like scorn, but which Neal could easily recognize as Blake's most vulnerable voice. "You're going to build a studio and it's in the country and you're going to record hipster albums. You think that's such a big deal, you can't go on tour with me?"

People were talking about him? If Blake was trying to make him feel bad about himself, this was not the way to do it.

Neal had to suppress another laugh.

Blake hated to be laughed at. He said: "Look man, I'm trying here. You just think this is funny?"

"Or," Neal said. "We could come down to Florida. March break? Sid and Nancy could go to Disney World."

"Fuck you," Blake said. "I forgot how petty you can be. You are the proudest person I ever met. You always said I have a big ego. But I'm nothing compared to you."

"Okay."

"Just remember the only reason you make any royalty money at all is because the band got big after you left."

"Yeah," Neal said. "I am aware of that."

"You leech."

"Merry Christmas, Blake," Neal said, and hung up.

It took a great effort to refrain from throwing the mugs full of eggnog up against the wall.

For a while he looked out the window. He tried to wrestle his thoughts back to his family, his property, his studio, but all those things seemed a little dirty to him now. His only satisfaction that he could tell, through the queer telepathy that came from knowing someone too long, that Blake was feeling the same way down in Florida, as he looked at the palm trees and the white sand and the blue sky, half-way across the world, floating in the boat paid for by all that shittily-reviewed nu-rock.

And then Neal noticed a funny thing. The door to the barn, to his studio, was slowly swinging open. Before his eyes. Yawning open, really, like a mouth. Despite that he'd locked it shut.

He thought about sending LaTanya or Sid out to lock the door. Not because he thought for a moment because he'd be putting them in danger, but because he thought she wouldn't come out for anyone but him. And because if she did come, at least he wouldn't be the only one who'd seen it.

He could go out with one of them, but then what if only he could see her? What if they thought he was going crazy? What if he was going crazy?

His mouth dried out and he swallowed.

"Babe?" LaTanya said, from right behind him.

He jumped.

"Oh, I'm sorry," she laughed, and looked at the mugs. A little too greedily, Neal couldn't help thinking. "Is it ready?" she asked.

"Yeah," Neal said. "Take 'em out to the kids. I have to go out there and close the door."

LaTanya looked past him through the window to the barn.

"The door is open!" she said.

"I know."

"Baby, why'd you leave the door open?"

She was always asking him questions like that. Why didn't you load the dishwasher? Why did you skid through that stop sign? Why didn't you put the shirt in the wrong drawer? Like nothing was ever an accident, and he did everything according to a secret plan to fuck with her.

"I forgot," he said.

She drew him to her and kissed him on the forehead. He trooped down to the mudroom like a condemned man, strapped on his expensive goretex boots and pulled on his The North Face parka.

Sid wandered up from the basement on his way to the kitchen. Sid was tall and stooped and quiet, with a big light-coloured afro that formed a halo around his head. He liked to build model airplanes and LaTanya was pretty sure that he'd recently discovered the joys of jacking off. To Neal's secret delight he showed no interest in becoming an artist.

"Did you make eggnog?" Sid asked.

"Yeah, go help yourself."

"Sweet."

"Hey Sid?"

"Yeah?"

"You still into ghosts?"

"No, not really," Sid said. "Why?"

"No reason," Neal said. "Do you know how to make a ghost go away?"

"Like if a house is haunted?"

"Yeah."

"Usually they aren't at rest because they weren't properly buried. Like they were murdered by someone and you need to find their bones and bury them in a churchyard."

"Right."

"Why do you ask?"

"No reason."

"Dad, you're being weird."

"That's me. Weird Dad."

It was bright outside, and dry, and cold. The path to the barn was not icy, but the snow was packed down so it was shiny and hard. All the lights in the barn were turned on, and there was the sound of music playing.

The lock was not on the door. He had to search for a while to find it. It had been thrown about five feet away from the path, where it had punched a hole in the snow. Neal dug around with his bare fingers and came up with it. His flesh cold and white and raw.

Hope was rising in him, the hope that he wouldn't see the ghost.

Inside he shut down all the recording equipment. It was colder inside than out, but that happened sometimes in old buildings like this. They were damp and dark. They could be drafty.

He was back outside in less than thirty seconds and then he closed the door and tried to snap the lock shut. It took a while because his hands were shaking. Because of the cold. After a moment he got it and looked up and something he saw stopped him.

It was the doe, still in the woods. Just standing there, not twenty feet away. Frozen unnaturally still, as if it was paralyzed, or stuffed. Looking past him with its dark, liquid eyes. At something behind him.

The air started getting colder and colder. Like he was in an elevator that was plummeting down into a very cold place. He closed his eyes and a couple of tears squeezed out. They froze on his cheeks. If he saw the ghost again he would die. He would almost rather it killed him without him having to see it.

Neal ...

It whispered in his ear, but he didn't get the feeling that it was close behind him. It was more as if the word had been wrapped in a cold breeze and had drifted into his ear from a long distance. He flinched a little, and gasped. And he turned around and saw her again.

She was walking across the snow with her back to him. The sunlight shone right through her transparent form. She cast no shadow. And again he had that feeling of pure terror, so hard and unyielding, it felt as if his heart would split, but once again he was also intoxicated with her beauty. The slender body clearly visible through the flimsy shift, with her narrow waist and wide hips and long legs. The curve of her breasts slightly visible under her crossed arms.

She didn't turn around but her shoulders were shaking like she was crying. He wanted to hold her, but he knew that his hands would move right through her. She was not real.

He bolted as fast as he could, but this time he had the self possession to slow down before he went back into the house, to open the door gently and close it the same way. Then he stood for a while in the mudroom, shaking badly, stamping his feet to draw out the warmth from the floor. It took him a while to still his heart.

Once he calmed down he peered through the window, expecting her to suddenly appear. But she didn't. So he walked up the stairs to where he could hear his children shouting and his wife laughing, his soul laden with a curious species of regret.

Paulus, his agent, was a thoroughly depressing person, with tattered clothes and an unconvincing comb-over and a thin layer of dandruff, or dust, on his shoulders. He had a pleading way of talking, even in regular conversation, as if he was so accustomed to begging he did it automatically. Now he was begging Neal to start renting out his studio.

"You know Neal, there really is a lot of interest out there now," Paulus said. "Going into nature to record a minimalist album, that's really the in thing these days. Just like Bon Iver. You know? I really think it's the trendy thing right now, and we should make hay while the sun shines."

In some ways it took a lot of courage to back into the studio, but in another he almost felt drawn there, like a fish getting reeled in.

He recorded a few of his new songs, experimented with some different instruments he'd picked up over the years. At the moment he was fascinated by the xylophone. He drank chamomile tea from a glass jam jar and alternated between listening to Thelonius Monk and dicking around with the xylophone, trying (and failing) to come up with a tune that didn't instantly conjure dancing skeletons to his mind. No luck, as far as he was concerned, but when he posted a video of himself on Youtube he had fifty thousand hits in no time, along with pages of adoring comments and an invitation (pathetically conveyed to him by Paulus) to jam at Arts & Crafts with some members of Broken Social Scene.

Every now and then it would get cold in the studio, or something would fall over. Nothing too overt, but still, he felt very uncomfortable. Like he was watched. He hated that feeling; he'd moved out of the city, at least in part, to get away from it. As soon as the snow melted he abandoned the studio and drove to Home Depot to get the bricks and mortar to build his barbeque pit.

While he was looking at lumber, a young man with a tight T-shirt and a pair of dark framed glasses walked up to talk to him.

"Hey man, look, I know you moved up here because you didn't want anyone to bug you, and I respect that ..."

No you don't, Neal thought.

"... but I just wanted to tell you I really dig your music."

Neal smiled and nodded.

"Thanks man."

Neal turned back to the wood but the young man kept talking.

"*Wild Garlic* is one of my top five albums."

"Glad you like it."

"No problem."

Neal smiled and started loading lumber onto his cart.

"Can I ask you something?" the young man asked.

"Sure."

"Does it bug you when people come up and tell you things like that? Or does it make you feel good?"

Neal stopped for a moment.

"I think I would miss it if they didn't do it," Neal said. "I always thought it would make me happy. But when it happens I usually just feel awkward."

"Sorry."

"It's okay," Neal said. "Feelings in real life are awkward."

"Yeah man."

"The only thing that really bugs me is when people tell me they were my fans back in the day," Neal said, "That's fucking bullshit. If one-twentieth of the people who said they were my fans back in the day were my fans back in the day, we'd have actually been popular. Believe me. I played those fucking shows. There was no one there."

"I wasn't your fan back in the day," the young man said. "I was only 13 when you quit the band."

"Yeah, but see," Neal said. "That just makes me feel old."

The young man laughed, and then waved at Neal's cart.

"Is this stuff for your studio?"

"No," Neal said. "I'm building something else."

"Cool," the young man said. "Well, have a nice day."

"You too."

A couple of middle-aged men in orange aprons helped him load everything into his truck. On the drive back he listened to one of the electronic radio stations he got through satellite radio. He liked jungle much better than rock and roll these days.

He drove around to his backyard where he was going to build the pit. While he was unloading the truck his wife came out and gave him a look, like she had something to tell him but she was worried it was going to give him a heart attack.

"What?"

"We got voice messages from a bunch of reporters."

"How do they always get our fucking number? I told that dumb slut Paulus ..."

"Oh Neal," she sighed, "I guess Blake is on tour and he's talking shit about you."

She held up their netbook so he could read the story but she did not hand it to him. No doubt she was still morbidly sensitive about the time he had he had put his bare foot through the screen of their old tube TV during Blake's Juno acceptance speech.

The Bards entertained the crowd with just about all of their biggest hits, but also sprinkled in a number of covers. Lead singer Blake Sale dedicated Wish You Were Here *by Pink Floyd to former bandmate Neal Adams, who, he said was going through "a very tough time" and was in "a very dark place." Sale asked the crowd to keep Adams in their prayers, so that he would be a great artist once again.*

"What the fuck?" Neal said, and reached for the computer, intending to smash it over his knee. LaTanya jerked it away. "What the fuck? That fucking cocksucker! He makes me sound like Syd fucking Barret! What a fucking asshole! What a piece of shit!"

"I know baby, I know," LaTanya said.

"That worthless dicksucking piece of trash!" Neal raged. His face had gone deep red. "That dirty Chad Kruger wannabe! He has the nerve to say I'm crazy because I don't want to go on tour and play his shitty music!"

LaTanya was already walking back to the house.

"Just thought you'd want to know," she said.

Neal turned his pile of bricks and he almost started punching them, but he didn't. Instead he stood in that empty wet field and choked back tears of helpless rage. He felt violated in his own home. He felt like he was getting pushed around by someone much bigger than he was. Someone he couldn't fight back against. He felt so small.

Eventually he wiped his eyes with the back of his hands and he made his way to the barn. For the rest of the afternoon he plunked out songs on his guitar. Songs with soul. CCR and Neil Young, the White Stripes and the Black Keys.

After a few hours her presence around him became so thick that he felt like if he stayed it would asphyxiate him, like how smoke will kill you before the fire in a burning house. It got so cold his fingers stumbled on the strings. His breath grew shorter, his heart started beating. He closed his eyes and kept playing. He knew, he just knew, she was behind him.

He didn't want to turn around and look at her. He couldn't. So he squeezed his eyes tighter and played, although his frozen fingers were tripping over the strings.

And then there was a cold burst in the nape of his neck, and he gasped, and he heard her melodious voice:

Neal ...

But when he turned around she wasn't there.

By the time he got inside and took the call from the reporter he knew exactly what he was going to say.

The questions started off easy, no, he wasn't crazy, yes, everything was fine, he had a house and a wife and kids and a normal life and he was quite happy now, thank you, whatever Blake said.

"You know," Neal said, "Blake and I were always very different people. And if the music we made together was any good, it was because of our differences, not in spite of them. That tension between us made our music good. When I left the band, and the bond between us broke, it was like we snapped off in totally different directions. He ended up where he is, and I ended up where I am. But we're both all right. Everything's okay."

"How do you mean?" the reporter asked.

Neal detected a faint note of anticipation in his voice.

"Well, let me tell you a story," Neal said, grinning as he jammed the phone in his ear. "About six months before I left the band we had a gig at a bar on Dundas and Ossington. We're opening for someone. Things have been tough for us for years. We get good reviews but we can't break through. You know the story. So Blake and I are getting drunk at the bar and we hit on this idea. We're only going to play Creed covers. That's it. We're drunk and we're laughing and we print up a bunch of lyrics and music sheets in the manager's office and then we get on the stage and start playing *Arms Wide Open*. Like, fuck all those hipsters, right? Only everyone started laughing and cheering. They're singing along. All these fucking hipsters that are too cool for school, they know the lyrics to every fucking Creed song. They're clapping and laughing and when it becomes clear that we aren't going to play any of our own music, any at all, they get into it more than ever. When we got off the stage everyone came up to us and told us how *awesome* we were, how *great* that was. Fucking chicks are all over us, okay? Seriously. We had played, I don't know, two hundred gigs and that was the biggest reaction we ever got."

And then the dagger:

"I just think Blake and I took totally different lessons from that experience."

The reporter could scarcely contain his glee.

You like that Blake? Neal thought grimly as he hung up. *I have a million stories like that. Stories about needy, whiny wannabe rock star Blake Sale. You want to get into it with me? Well, good fucking luck. Because it's you they're after, not me. Throwing me under the bus doesn't sell papers. I'm just a crazy guy in Northumberland County. You're their fucking whipping boy. It's what you wanted. Now you fucking got it.*

Within hours the story was on the newspaper's website, then it hit the blogs, and then it started making the rounds on the social media.

"Poor Blake," LaTanya said when they were in bed that night.

"What the fuck do you mean?" Neal said.

"I just can't help but feel sorry for him."

"He's a fucking millionaire!" Neal said.

"Oh, yes, I know," LaTanya said. "And he brings it on himself. But he's not strong like you are, Neal. So I feel sorry for him, sometimes."

Within a few minutes LaTanya was snoring gently. Neal couldn't sleep. He sat up and put his feet down on the cold floor and stared out the window. He didn't like to admit it, but he was looking for the ghost.

The barbeque pit was a big success. Sid, in particular, loved it, and was always looking on the Internet for new things to smoke and new kinds of wood to smoke with. Neal considered starting a restaurant. Like one of those places in Georgia where people would drive an hour outside of Atlanta to a little hole-in-the-wall. But he let that go, to drift down the current with all the rest of the things he could have done in his life.

Eventually he had to give in and let Paulus send somebody up to play in the studio. The band was called *Dinosaur Bones*, and they were big on the local scene. They were coming up to record their first full-length album, and everyone talked about them like the next sure thing. Neal had been the next sure thing too long for that to mean anything to him.

So they showed up, five shaggy haired kids in clothes that had been carefully chosen to appear casually chosen. They were very deferential to Neal, they were polite to LaTanya, they were fun with the kids. They loved the property, they raved about the barbeque, they were in ecstasy over the studio. They set Neal's teeth on edge.

Like most of the new wave of rockers, they were much more dedicated to their craft than those of Neal's generation. While Neal had been skipping school and working in his stepfather's garage, and while Blake had been dodging dishes hurled at him by his schizophrenic mother, these kids had all been in band camp, learning to play the oboe and the clarinet at their parents' expense. Blake claimed they were technically proficient but lacked heart. Neal was pretty sure they were just better. All of this was to say they didn't get drunk the first night and were ready to go very early the next morning.

They had a "producer" with them from whatever bullshit indie label had signed them, and he was pretty snippy around Neal. Neal would have been content to leave him in charge, but the band really wanted him in the studio, so he filled up a thermos with peppermint tea and brought a copy of *The Economist* and sat in the back room and offered opinions when anyone asked.

It was a disaster. There was one technical problem after another. Stuff for which there was just no explanation. Guitar strings kept snapping. The power went on and off. It was unpleasantly cold. And the few recordings they made all had odd background noise.

"Turn it up," Dave the keyboardist said, while they were listening to one recording. "Turn it up. Does that sound like someone crying to you?"

After two days of this the band had a "meeting" and the producer came up and started getting aggressive about it.

"Relax," Neal said. "You can have your money back."

Perhaps disappointed he wasn't going to be able to make a fight out of it, the manager said:

"It's fucking amateur for you to call us out here when your shit isn't ready to go."

Neal smiled and said:

"Well, we're all amateurs here. Aren't we?"

And so that was that. Neal told LaTanya and the kids not to take Paulus's calls for a few days. He was very quiet and they gave him a fair amount of space. Neal didn't know how to feel. Part of him was a little amused. Part of him was even a bit relieved that it hadn't gone well. The hype that had been building in certain circles around this project had been stressing him out more than he'd care to admit. But another part was frustrated and sad. And trapped.

He called the Realtor to get the history of who had owned the property when. After a couple of days in the library looking at newspapers on microfiche, he found the ghost. Her name was Jane MacPherson, and she'd vanished back in 1907. Her husband had been interviewed by the police but nothing had come of it. Her picture was in the paper. She looked like something wild and lost, even then. Her eyes burned across a hundred years.

When he came back home he went into the kitchen and started making dinner. He did not go to the barn. He only looked at it through the window.

They'd been in Northumberland County for a year and they were past due to start having some family over. Neal and LaTanya talked about it and decided the best thing was throw a big shin-dig and get it all out of the way at once. So they cleaned and scrubbed and rented dishes and lawn furniture and set everything up for a big family barbeque on the August long weekend. Neal bought pork shoulder and sides of beef and whole chickens, made four different sauces, and worked the barbeque for 24 hours in advance.

The morning of the big day Neal pulled his kids into the solarium and gave them a lecture. There really was no need, his kids were always good, but he always thought it was best to set expectations.

"All right. You guys be on your best behaviour. Sid, if I see you dicking around with the PSP or anything like that, I'm going to take it away for the rest of the summer. Talk to your cousins. Nancy, if me or mom tells you to give someone a break, then give them a break. People can't play with you all the time. Grownups get tired faster than you."

"You don't get tired," Nancy said. She was seven and as skinny as a rail. Her teeth pointed in all different directions, like a herd of cattle that had scattered, but otherwise she was as cute as a button.

"Oh, I get tired," Neal said. "I get more tired than you can imagine. Anyway, if you're both good, I'll get you a Kinect."

This had the desired effect. Nancy jumped up and screeched.

The invitation for was for 1 pm, but predictably, LaTanya's parents showed up at 11:30. They were blue collar Jamaican immigrants from Scarborough, deeply traditional, and they had had LaTanya very young. They were both fat and they had always loathed Neal. First he had been in the band that wasn't going anywhere, and now he was the idiot how had thrown away the golden ticket.

Neal invited them to take a seat in the living room, saying that he still had some work to do.

"Not so fast," LaTanya's father said. His name was Jake. "I got a bone to pick with you."

Neal froze on the way out of the room and raised one eyebrow.

"I want to know just what the hell you think you're doing turning down all that money to go on tour with your old band."

"Dad!" LaTanya said, horrified.

There was an ominous silence while Neal and Jake looked at each other. Jake sat on his fat ass on Neal's leather furniture, wearing a sanctimonious expression that clearly indicated he had no idea how close he was to being grievously injured.

"What?" Neal said.

"You heard me," Jake said. "Just who do you think you are, turning down all that money to go on tour? You're making my family suffer for your pride. I just want to get it right out of the way; I don't think you're doing right by my grandkids."

"Dad, shut the fuck up!" LaTanya screamed. She was sort of hugging herself in the extremity of her emotion.

"I'm not going to discuss this with you," Neal said. He felt as if he was watching two people argue on television. "You're a guest in my home. Keep your opinions to yourself, or you can get out."

"I'm going to speak my mind," Jake said. "LaTanya's told us how you think you're too good for your old buddy and you like to make fun of him. Well, he's the one with all the money. I think ..."

Neal crossed the distance to Jake in two steps and caught him by the throat with one hand and squeezed. Jake's eyes popped out of his head.

How times changed. When they had first met Jake had been 38, powerful, while Neal had been a malnourished 24-year-old rocker. Now they were 42 and 56, and for the past eighteen years Neal had eaten quinoa and done push-ups while Jake had decomposed on his couch.

"You will shut the fuck up," Neal screamed, "when you are in my home, or I will throw your fat ass out!"

"Stop it, stop it!" LaTanya's mother screamed.

LaTanya, for her part, did not say a word.

Neal tossed Jake onto the ground with one hand. Then he turned and looked at LaTanya, just looked at her, and she wilted. He stomped off into their bedroom, waited for her to follow, and then slammed the door behind her.

"What the fuck?" he hissed.

"Neal, I'm so sorry," LaTanya said. "I was just talking to my mom about it. I didn't say you did anything wrong."

"Well, what the fuck did you say?" Neal said. "You sure as shit said something!"

"I just said that he called and asked you to go on tour."

"And?" Neal said.

"And nothing."

"What do you mean, and nothing?"

"I didn't say you were too proud, or you were hurting the kids. My dad just made that up."

"Well, why are you telling your mom about this?" Neal said. "What were you thinking?"

"Neal, I'm sorry," LaTanya said. "You're so tense all the time. I just want you to be happy. Music's so important to you. I just thought it would maybe be good for you."

"Good for me?" Neal shouted. The depth of what he was feeling was astonishing to him. "Good for me? To go on tour with The Bards? To play bass on all of Blake's shitty songs? In all those fucking arenas in front of all those fucking idiots in their stupid skull-covered $100 t-shirts? To watch him do coke for hours on end? It would be good for me? Do you even know the first thing about who I am? How could you be so fucking stupid?"

She broke; her head dropped down to her chest and she started sobbing without reservation, her breasts hitching up and down. Making little wails of despair.

Neal thought: *You win! Good for you, asshole.*

He looked around their bedroom, for a while. The flatscreen TV on the wall, with five hundred channels. The king-sized bed, the sheets with 600 single-ply threads-per-inch, the iPod dock, the fancy alarm clock. The window looking out on their massive property. More than you should ever need to be happy, really.

He felt very, very tired, and so he squatted down and sat on his heels for a moment and listened to his wife cry.

"I'm sorry," she sobbed. "I'm so sorry!"

Neal stood up and hugged her for a while.

"I'm so sorry," she said.

"Stop saying that," he said.

"I'm so sorry," she wailed. "I'm so sorry. I just want you to be happy."

"Stop it, stop it," he said. He had to bite back tears. His broken fucking life. God. "Just stop. It's okay. It's okay. Never you mind. All right? Don't you mind. All right? It's okay. Everything is okay. Never you mind."

LaTanya was normally pretty good about putting on a front for other people when she was feeling upset or angry or just bitchy. But she was shaken, and it showed. For his part, Neal was terrible at hiding his emotions and it was clear that something was wrong with him. The kids were traumatized. And so the barbeque was strained and awkward, fully of gloomy silences as the guests looked at each other and mutely speculated whether LaTanya and Neal's marriage was breaking up. The whole thing was a disaster long before Sid saw the ghost.

Parents listen to their children make all sorts of loud noises and they swiftly gain the ability to tell if something is serious. Neal was tersely talking to LaTanya's cousin Jeff about the Leafs' chances next year when they heard a thin scream come from the barn. It was a serious scream.

Neal dropped his beer bottle onto the lawn where it fizzed and overflowed and he sprinted as fast as he could, feeling a kind of real terror that he hadn't felt in a very long time. He threw open the barn door and saw his son lying flat on the ground, his face yellowish and waxy.

"I don't know what happened!" the other kid said. "We weren't doing anything!"

Neal gathered Sid up in his arms and carried him back to the house.

"It's okay, Sid," Neal said. "It's okay."

Sid's lips were trembling. There were tears in his eyes.

"Daddy," he squeaked.

"Shh, shh, be strong."

"I saw a ghost," he sobbed.

"I know you did, I know you did. You're safe."

Neal carried him outside and up the path to the back door under the gaze of thirty of his relatives, who helpfully started to hover around and panic.

"He's fine," Neal said. "He's fine."

"What happened?" LaTanya shrieked.

"He's fine," Neal said.

"What happened?" LaTanya said.

"Let me get him inside and I'll tell you about it."

"What happened to him?" she shrieked, again.

"Mommy," Sid said.

At this point they were standing at the sliding glass door that led into the back of the house. Everyone was crowding around without making a move to open it.

"LaTanya," Neal said, striving to keep the anger out of his voice, "open the door."

Once they were inside Neal carried Sid into his bedroom and tucked him in.

"I'm so cold," Sid said, crying. "It got really cold. Even Brad said so. We could see our breath. Then I saw her. She was really scary looking."

"Shh, shh," Neal said.

"Who's he talking about?" LaTanya said.

"He says he saw a ghost," Neal said. "He's just scared. He's not hurt."

"I did see her," Sid said. "She was real."

"I believe you," Neal said.

Sid was calming down but his eyes were full of tears and he was sobbing and he looked very miserable.

"She looked really scary," Sid said. "I don't think she was mad at me. She was really pretty. But she looked so scary. I can't even describe it. What if she comes back?"

"She won't," Neal said. "I'll take care of her."

"How?" Sid said.

"I will," Neal said. "I promise."

And then he stood up and hugged his wife.

"Why don't you stay with him?" Neal said. "I'll go see about everybody."

"Nice party," she said.

He smiled. It was just the muscles in his mouth moving, without anything behind it.

That night he couldn't sleep. Around midnight he got hungry. He'd been so upset and so busy that he hadn't eaten very much. There were plenty of leftovers. Beef brisket and smoked chicken and pulled pork, along with all the coleslaw and potato salad. The thought of it made his stomach rumble.

So he got up and padded into the kitchen and made a little plate for himself. It was in the oven, covered in tinfoil, when he heard her voice.

Neal.

Like a knot of cold air unravelling in his ear.

He looked out the window and she was standing right there, the same thin cotton dress clinging to her perfect body. Her hands were clasped underneath the globes of her breasts and her hair was blowing, even though there was no wind. He could see the trees through her, and the stars.

Neal, she said again, but her lips didn't move.

And then she faded away, like a haze of smoke clearing.

"Dad?"

Neal turned around. It was Sid.

"Hey Sid. Can't sleep?"

Sid shook his head. He looked like he was going to cry.

"You hungry?"

Sid shook his head again.

"Okay, well, sit down, I'll be there in a second."

Neal took his plate out of the oven with a dishtowel and set it on a thick place matt on the table, and then he sat down next to Sid.

"You all right bud?"

"Dad, you believe me, right?"

"Yeah, I believe you."

"I didn't think you would believe in ghosts."

Neal didn't say anything. He took the foil off of the plate and picked up a forkful of pork.

"But you asked me about ghosts back in the winter."

Neal put the pork in his mouth, although he had lost his appetite.

"Have you seen her?" Sid said.

After a moment, Neal said: "Yeah, I saw her."

"Why didn't you say anything?"

"I didn't want you to think I was crazy."

"But we could have seen her too."

"Well, she's not much to look at."

Sid looked away.

"It's all right," Neal said.

"Are you going to get rid of her?"

"Yes."

Sid started to cry.

"Why didn't you do it already? I told you back at Christmas. I can't ever unsee that, Dad."

"I'm sorry Sid."

"Whatever," Sid said, and wiped his eyes. "I'll never get over this."

"Teenagers never think they'll get over anything," Neal said. "Go to bed. You're safe. I'll take care of it."

Sid stood up and wiped his eyes some more.

"Can you come with me?" he asked hoarsely.

Neal pushed his plate away.

"All right," he said. "I kind of lost my appetite anyway."

They talked about video games for a while. They both detested *Rock Band* and *Guitar Hero*. Eventually Sid fell asleep. Neal left the light on but closed the door most of the way and then went back into the kitchen and looked out at the barn. He felt the same kind of resentment he'd been feeling before, but stronger this time.

Enough.

His neighbour Tom was a sergeant with the Ontario Provincial Police Emergency Response Team, or, as he preferred to call it, the OPP ERT. He was tall, lean, and quiet, almost totally bald with a small, neat moustache. Tom worked four days on and four days off and so he was often free during the middle of the week to hang out.

Neal called him and asked him to go out mountain biking. It was a beautiful day for it, and it was nice to get some hard exercise, to sweat out the regret and frustration that seemed to have burrowed under his skin. They took a break at the top of a steep hill, with the mosquitoes humming around them and the birds calling from the branches, and Neal said:

"I have a big favour to ask of you."

"Shoot," Tom said.

"And you can't talk shit about it, or ask any questions."

"Hmm."

"I'm serious."

"Well, go ahead."

"I need you to get one of your buddies to come over with one of those ground penetrating radar machines to have a look around my barn."

Tom's eyebrows shot up. He started to look pretty wry.

"I'm serious," Neal said. "No questions. Tell him I'll get him two bottles of whatever he wants. I just need him to run it around in there."

"All right, Neal," Tom said.

Two days later Bill and Tom drove up in a gleaming Ford pickup. Bill was short and squat, like a fire hydrant, clean shaven with a crisp grey crew cut. He was wearing a white sleeveless t-shirt and a tattoo of a squid was on his left arm. Neal handed over two bottles of Crown Royal, which he privately felt demonstrated a rather serious lack of imagination on Bill's part, and they unloaded the GPR from his truck. It looked a lot like a lawn-mower, only with a monitor on the handlebar.

"Okay," Bill said. "Now if we're going to do this, there's something we've got to get straight right from the beginning."

"Okay," Neal said.

"Tom may have promised not to talk shit about this," Bill said. "But that does not apply to me."

And then the cracks started. Bill slowly pushed the GPR around the barn and unleashed one witticism after another: wondering whether Neal wasn't turning into Ozzy Osbourne, speculating as to the quality of the peyote Neal been ingesting, enquiring if Neal merely needed to learn the true meaning of Christmas, issuing warnings that they could be "slimed" at any moment, and so forth. Tom trailed behind Bill giggling.

Neal leaned against the front door. He had a crow bar tucked under his arm. A shovel was in the corner.

Bill started to ask whether they maybe didn't need to get Whoopi Goldberg in here, and then he stopped short in the far rear corner of the barn, in the studio proper, and looked at his monitor.

"That's odd," he said.

"Okay," Neal said, and walked over. "Thanks bud."

"It's probably nothing," Bill said. "I don't know that you want to tear your floor up over it."

"I'm pretty sure I do," Neal said.

He ripped out the floor boards quickly and then took up the shovel.

"Is it cold in here?" Tom asked.

"Yep," Neal said, and when he exhaled, he could see his breath.

With every spadeful of earth he lifted out of the ground the wind seemed to howl louder. After a few minutes it sounded like someone was screaming. It was so cold that Neal had to clench his teeth to keep them from chattering.

Finally Neal lifted up one scoop of dirt and planted it on the mound, and a very pale white bone tumbled loose.

"That's enough," Bill said.

The wind outside was gone. It was warming up.

"Don't you think we better get her all the way out?" Neal said.

"Sure," Bill said. "But it's time to call this one in. Go on inside Mr. Adams. Someone'll be in to talk to you soon."

"Okay," Neal said, and leaned the shovel up against the wall.

"Is this all a joke, Neal?" Tom said.

"Nope," Neal said.

"How'd you know the body was there?" Tom asked.

"I didn't," Neal said. "That's why I brought you boys over."

"Neal," Tom said. "How'd you know a body was here at all?"

"Never mind," Neal said.

"Is this a joke? Did you make it colder in here?"

"See you, Tom," Neal said. "I'm going inside."

On the walk up the path he felt like he was being watched, but it gave him some satisfaction to know that soon that feeling would be gone.

When the police asked him for a statement he told them he was exercising his right to remain silent, and recommended they go do the forensic work. The bones turned out to have been buried for a hundred years. Neal never made a statement about it, public or private. Everyone assumed it was a publicity stunt, because, well, what was the alternative?

If it had been a publicity stunt, it had certainly worked. The reporters were all over them, a thousand times worse than they had been before. The manager for Dinosaur Bones called and begged for their recordings. Paulus was ecstatic; if Neal wanted, the studio could be booked for two years solid. Leslie Feist, Joel Plaskett and Gord Downey were among those who'd called. Hell, even K-OS and Kardinall Offishall wanted to come up and screw around.

At $2,000 a day. Shit.

Blake called him one night, from Columbus Ohio. He was coked to the gills and laughing at his own jokes but it was still the best conversation they'd had since about three months before the band broke up. It was probably just the drugs, but Blake said something about coming up and renting the studio and recording a song. Caught by surprise, Neal said sure.

"Fire up the barbeque!" Blake shouted.

The only downside was that Tom never quite forgave Neal. They kept biking together but Tom was only civil. Probably Tom wouldn't have minded if the whole thing had been a prank, he wasn't without a sense of humour, but he couldn't tolerate the ambiguity. As a police officer, he detested mystery.

Neal got tired of the xylophone and started playing around with a ukulele. He recorded a lot of Jack Johnson covers and put them on YouTube, thoroughly enjoying all the online speculation about whether he was trying to be ironic or sell out or had just gone crazy.

Halfway through his rendition of *What You Thought You Need*, it got a little colder. And he felt the presence behind him.

Curious, he turned around, and saw the ghost standing above the place where her bones had lain for so long. She wasn't frightening any more. She was faint, just a hazy outline, and she was flickering like a thin flame on a windy night.

"What are you doing back here?" he said.

And she spoke to him without moving her lips, in that windy voice that seemed to be coming from a long ways away.

Neal, she whispered. *I didn't visit you because I wasn't at rest, because I wanted to be buried in a churchyard. I came back for you. I loved you.*

Neal had a sensual mouth, like Tim Curry, or the Emperor Nero, and he could look quite cruel when he frowned, which he did now.

"You don't think I knew that?" Neal said. "I always knew about you. Go away. I love my wife. I'm happy with my life. Go away to wherever you're supposed to be, and leave me alone."

Neal went back to his ukulele. He felt the room get warmer and he didn't need to look up to know that the ghost was gone, for good this time.

It was fall now. The kids got home from school and LaTanya came back from work and they had had homemade pizza for dinner. Afterwards Nancy practiced her violin and Sid painted his Warhammer figurines and LaTanya went downstairs to catch up on some episodes of *The Amazing Race* she had PVR'd. Her deep laughter floated up to where he was sitting on the back patio. The wind rustled and the crickets hummed. It was still very light out, but it was darkening, and cool. Neal drank raspberry tea and looked at the trees. It's a good thing to let go of your ghosts.

3 The thing that lives in traffic

Everyone who knows me knows about my aversion to traffic. I won't drive on a major highway anywhere near rush hour. I come into work before dawn, and I usually go home before my colleagues have lunch. If I can't leave early, I stay till after sunset. I take zigzagging, roundabout routes over lonely, abandoned country roads. I eat my meals at irregular hours to avoid lines, I leave hockey games halfway through the third period, and I take my family on vacation in November.

But then everyone hates traffic. The tedium of it coupled with the dreadful consciousness that you could be going so much faster. And its caprice. It's like some kind of sick game, or a living thing. It changes, moves, now in one place, now in another, now for ten minutes, now for thirty. Even when things are good, you're afraid, you can't relax.

We all run from traffic, hide from it, plan around it, and so my behavior is only a little outside the norm. But if my friends and family knew why I am so frightened of traffic, they would not consider me just a little kooky. They would think I'm completely insane, and so will you, when you read these pages. But if you're reading them, I must have died in a traffic accident, just like Andy did. Perhaps I was run off the road when someone didn't check their blind spot, or struck by a drunk driver while I was walking along the sidewalk, or was jostled off the platform in front of an oncoming train. Considering what you're about to read, it was a pretty big coincidence for me to die like that. But then, there are a thousand ways to die on your commute, and I'm sure you'd rather believe in unlikely coincidences then this story.

I am, by trade, an accountant. I came up with Ersnt & Young but I got tired of that life around the time I got married, so I joined a smaller firm at Yonge and St. Clair. My wife and I rented an apartment on Mount Pleasant, a big sprawling condo in an older building with a huge balcony.

During those years I was barely conscious of traffic at all. Everything I needed, including work, was within a five minute walk. We didn't own a car until the birth of our first child, and even then we barely used it. Certainly we would never venture out on the roads during peak periods. I realize now, with hindsight, that I had learned so well to avoid traffic that I was able to almost forget that it existed.

But all good things must come to an end. When our second child was born, my wife told me flatly that we needed to buy a house. We put in offers on four places but were outbid each time. Shitty little bungalows way out east that would have stuck me with a forty five minute commute were selling for close to a million dollars.

My wife insisted we go look at a place in Guelph. Eventually I went just to please her. The first place we looked at was a mansion, right downtown, with a stone wall around the yard, big cathedral windows, slick dark hardwood floors, all new appliances, and a 16 x 40 pool in the backyard. It was well within our budget. My wife was in love. I had some reservations about the commute, but I fooled myself that it wouldn't be so bad.

"We're going to live here?" my son kept saying. "Really? Here?"

My wife found a job in Kitchener, but I had made partner at my firm, and quitting wasn't in the cards, not with our mortgage. My commuting days had begun.

And what a monster, what an absolute whore, that commute was. I left at 6:30 a.m. my first day but the Hanlon was already crowded. Congestion increased after I got on the 401, though I was able to keep the needle around 100 until the Guelph Line exit, where I was confronted with a hateful wall of bright red taillights. For a while we moved slowly, like thoughtful school of fish, until we came to the next exit, where we stopped and sat in agonizing boredom for a few minutes. Things momentarily eased up after every exit, and then tightened up again, getting worse and worse as the 401 wound through the city.

The Allen Expressway was a parking lot, especially where it ended at Eglinton, and driving across town was a nightmare, with buses stopping every fifty feet, jaywalkers darting suicidally across the road, and cars waiting forever to turn left. The kicker was when I arrived at work and realized that parking would cost me $20 for the day.

I spent the last hour of the day refreshing Google maps, looking desperately for some path that wasn't controlled by the enemy. Should I take Mount Pleasant to the 401? Head back to the Allan? Go east to the DVP? Cut my way through the backroads? I tried the latter strategy but every road was clotted and choked like the arteries of a man having a heart attack.

When I got home, my wife told me I'd figure it out. But I never did. When you try to outsmart traffic, you're really trying to outsmart all the other drivers, but they're as desperate to be out of the congestion as you are. You have to just accept it, or else you'll go crazy.

Around the time I was learning to do just that, I met Andy, our next-door neighbor.

I got to talking to him when I came home. He was watering his front lawn, wearing shorts and a white undershirt that was stained with, at best, mustard. Although it was only 7 pm, he was clearly a little drunk. But he turned out to be a pretty sharp lawyer. I gave him the general details of a problem one of our clients was having, and he did a better job breaking it down in five minutes than the over-billing no-nothing who was on the file had been able to do in 11.4 hours.

After that I got the feeling that he waited for me to show up every evening so he could shoot the breeze about downtown life. Despite his haggard face and his dirty grey hair, he was only in his forties. His wife had left him and taken their two high-school-aged kids, and I gathered that he had suffered some sort of a mental break. He must have been very lonely. My wife told me he barely left the house. She pitied him, but avoided him too. I think she thought his bad luck might be catching, and the way things turned out, I guess she was right.

Sometimes he'd invite me inside. The place was a mess of papers and maps but he had a great scotch collection. I usually only stayed about 15 minutes, but he'd always be noticeably drunker before I left.

Every time we spoke he asked me in an unusually dark tone how I was finding the commute.

When I heard he was behind in his child support, I started trying to feed him some work. I was able to flip him a few small things, and he was pitifully grateful, like dog watching you eat with big eyes and whimpering under its breath. I resolved to try and get him something pretty good, if I could, maybe something to coax him back into the city.

It wasn't long before something came up. One of our clients had lost a big trial and they were very unhappy with how their lawyers had handled it. They wanted someone new for the appeal and they were ready to pay a flat fee of $30,000.

I ran the idea past Andy, and I could tell he was excited. But he was very worried about traffic. He told me he'd have to take the train around lunchtime, when traffic was lowest, and stay the night before the appeal in a hotel. When I told him the client wanted to meet him face to face, at first he wanted them to come out to Guelph to see him, and only agreed to go to Toronto if the meeting was in the middle of the day, and not too long, so he could get in, and get out, without getting caught up in rush hour.

"I don't drive in rush hour anymore," he said.

"Not even for thirty grand?" I asked.

"Not for your life," he said.

Unfortunately, the day before the meeting I got an e-mail from the client asking to move it to 9 a.m. And they weren't asking, they were telling.

I broke the bad news to Andy in person, offering to drive him in myself, and to take him back right after lunch, so he wouldn't get stuck in traffic twice.

Nothing I'd seen had prepared me for his reaction; he jerked like he'd been stung and started shouting that wasn't part of the deal. When it became clear I wasn't going to let him off the hook, he started to beg. I mean literally beg. Tears in his eyes, his voice breaking up, his whole body shaking. He looked as if he was going to collapse with emotion.

I promised to get up very early to drive him in before rush hour (we'd have to leave at five) and he seemed to calm down a bit. But I was a little unsettled. I'd recommended this guy to an important client and I was starting to worry he was going to crack and make me look bad.

At 10 p.m., someone started banging on the front door. It was Andy, wild-looking, his hair standing up and his eyes bloodshot. He was almost crying again, babbling about how dangerous traffic was, how I wouldn't believe him but he'd written me a letter, which he was urging me to take, about what he'd learned during the three years he'd commuted to Toronto. He begged me to put the meeting off.

But I wasn't in the mood for it. I was thirty-six years old with a big mortgage and a young family and a fancy job in midtown Toronto. My crazy neighbor had woken up the baby and dollars-to-doughnuts he was going to embarrass the shit out of me tomorrow. I'm ashamed to admit it but I lost my temper. I told him he could back out of the whole deal if he wanted but otherwise he better be ready to go tomorrow at five. Andy lowered his head and trudged home without giving me the letter.

I try to tell myself that it wouldn't have made a difference, but I was seventeen minutes late picking up Andy the next morning. When I saw his face, stiff and waxy with fear, I cursed myself for making things worse. But I reassured myself there was no way we would hit traffic. Not even the Allan is busy before 6:30. We'd be fine.

But of course it was not to be. We turned around a corner on the Hanlon and came upon a snarl of cars jammed up bumper to bumper, blocking us from the next light.

"Oh, you're kidding me," I said.

"Oh my God," Andy said.

"I'm sorry Andy," I said.

"How can this be happening?" Andy shrieked, loud and painful in my ear. I looked over him, startled, and saw that he was gripping the armrests and his unnaturally old face was twisted with fear.

I felt a wave of compassion. This was a full blown phobia. I'd been so wrapped up in my own worries that I'd totally disregarded it.

"It's okay," I said. "Forget it. We'll call in sick and figure it out."

"You don't understand," Andy cried. A sour, old man smell of pure panic was coming off of him. "It found me! It's going to kill me!"

"Andy, calm down," I said. "We're just sitting here."

But he bolted like a spooked horse, unlocking the door and unbuckling his seat belt and fleeing.

"Andy!" I shouted.

We were in the left lane, and so to get off of the road, Andy had to circle around the car to our right. A horn blared, the sound of it enormous. I looked behind us just in time to see a truck barrel into the stalled line of cars in the right lane. The shock of the impact travelled through one car to the next, crumbling them like cans, and plastering Andy between an SUV and a large panel van.

I was out of the car in an instant. I won't get into the gory details but he was locked in a trap of bent and twisted metal. There was nothing I could do except hold his hand, get his blood all over my expensive suit, and lie to him and say everything would be fine.

The fear had gone out of his eyes and miraculously he didn't seem to be in much pain. No matter how many times I told him to just relax, to wait for the ambulance, he kept trying to say something. It took me a while to realize what it was.

"Don't read the letter," he kept saying. "Don't read the letter."

I took the day off work, and the next one. It was tough getting back in the car again. I think the only way that any of us find the courage to do it at all is to forget about the dangers of driving, and being in an accident makes that tough.

But I needed to get back to work, needed to pay for that house, to take care of my family. So I headed back out onto those roads so crowded with so many people driving at such high speeds, inches away from each other, seconds away from death. I drove into the maw of the city, again and again.

No one writes about the heroism of the 21st century commute, or its horrors. We prefer less ordinary stories. But it's the ordinary that's really out to get you. It's the ordinary that kills you, in the end.

About a week later the letter from Andy was mixed in with the mail when I came home from work. Unopened. My wife said that Mrs. Andy had dropped it off. I held it in my hands, feeling sick with regret and survivor's guilt, and then I opened it. Of course I did.

The letter read as follows:

I know you won't believe this but you're the only friend I've got, and I have to tell someone or I'll go crazy. Of course, you'll think I'm crazy already when you read this, but I swear to you, I'm not.

I was like you once, a young professional who wanted a bigger home than I could afford in Toronto. I knew the commute was going to be tough, but how hard could it be to figure out the optimal route and the optimal time? I made maps, kept a journal, studied the internet. After a while, I started to notice a pattern. It seemed that the traffic would, in general, get worse and worse until around the time of the new moon, and then it would suddenly drop off.

But what could I do with that? As you're finding out, there's no good way to do that commute, short of travelling well outside of anything approaching normal working hours. The traffic is everywhere; like a toxic gas that spreads into every available space. Day after day I found myself sitting in my car, trapped and powerless, like a pig being marched into the slaughterhouse.

One day, around the time of the new moon, traffic was particularly horrible, and I can remember the release I was aching for came right while I was sitting in my car. The river of red lights in my path blinked out, and the cars started to move, like an ice floe breaking up, or an army routing. My spirit soared, and at that moment, I got a call from my eldest boy. I put it on speaker. He was panicky; he'd just witnessed a car strike a pedestrian near his school. I calmed him down, told him the traffic was better and I'd be home soon.

An odd, unsettled feeling came over me, though. You will say it's crazy, but I couldn't help but wonder whether there was a connection between the fatal accident and the traffic starting to move.

Do you know what causes traffic jams, in the absence of an accident or construction? It isn't just congestion itself. After all, there is no reason why cars can't drive quickly with little space between them. It's a wave effect. When car decelerates, for whatever reason (perhaps another vehicle cutting in front of it,) the car following it has to decelerate a little harder (because our reflexes are not instantaneous). Then the car following that car has to brake even harder, and so forth. Eventually someone has to stop entirely. And when that car eventually gets moving again, the car behind it has to wait an extra moment to accelerate, and so forth.

All this is to say is that traffic spreads like a ripple on a pond. Who knows how far the ramifications of a seemingly simple thing can spread? I just couldn't let go of the instinctive suspicion that the death witnessed by my son was what released the gridlock on the 401.

That night I had terrible nightmares: I was hunted by something enormous and old. It was all around me, no matter which way I turned, looming, formless, foul. Eventually I realized that it had already eaten me, and I was in its belly. I screamed so loud I woke up people in the next house.

The next weekend, I began to cross-reference my traffic journals with reports of fatal accidents. At first I didn't see much of a pattern, but when I broadened my search to include anyone killed during rush hour, whether they were a pedestrian, a motorist, or a cyclist, something undeniable emerged. It was clear that someone always died right around the time that the traffic let up, around the time of the new moon.

If you want to see all this, I have the papers in my office. But I know they don't prove anything. I know that. Ultimately, you're going to have to take what happened next on faith.

I was on my regular morning commute, and I'd gotten away a little late, so it was a bad one. I came up over that hill around Guelph Line where things usually let up a little, but there was nothing but an unbroken ribbon of stopped cars and trucks stretching out as far as I could see. And so I sighed and sat back and stared at the taillights of the truck in front of me. There were twelve of them, set at different levels, and to me they looked a little like the beady and inhuman eyes of a spider.

And then suddenly it changed. It was like looking at one of those Magic Eye pictures, where your perspective shifts and something pops out. I saw a hideous monster in the traffic. The cars, the smoke and exhaust, the lights, the road itself, all of it together was like an enormous beast, a creature, a dark god. I saw it, I swear to you, but worse than that it saw me.

I screamed. I screamed right at the top of my lungs.

Somewhere behind me, one vehicle rear-ended another. The force of the collision travelled forward and the car behind me gave me a little tap. A coincidence? No. The thing was looking for me, fumbling around and trying to crush the life out of me.

I wanted to run, but where could I go? At that hour, traffic ruled. There was not a road I could take that wouldn't be rammed with cars, and wherever traffic was, I knew that this thing would be waiting for me.

Eventually, almost reluctantly, the traffic let go. I drove as carefully as I could, leaving lots of space in front of me, but I was still almost hit by a car cutting across from the far left hand lane to exit onto the 407. When I tried to overtake a slow moving truck it suddenly merged into my lane, and I had to stomp on the gas to avoid being swept off the road. And when I tried to walk from my parking spot to the office, I was almost hit by a cab running a red light.

And the monster was glaring at me, from every crowded bus, from every streetlight, from the thick crowds of pedestrians at the street corners. It stared at me! Wherever I went. Hungry for my blood.

On the commute home it was the same thing, one near miss after another. I can't describe how terrifying it was. How easily this thing could kill me! No one would suspect a thing. We put our lives in the hands of strangers every time we set out on our commute. Travelling at that speed, in machines of that weight. Why, any of us could die at any time. Now something was hunting me, hidden in all that noise and chaos, and there was no one I could tell.

I have often wondered about the nature of the thing that lives in traffic. My best guess is that it is some sort of old god. Men used to have a god for everything. A god of war, a god of the harvest, a god of childbirth. All those old gods have been lost and forgotten now. First there were the new gods, bright clean watchmakers who set the universe running and then stepped back, disinterested in sacrifice. Following on their heels was science, which provided dependable solutions to all problems, making sacrifice unnecessary.

And so the old gods fell into dust, except for one. For all the problems we've solved, traffic has gotten worse, and not better. Perhaps the god of traffic was forgotten, but it did not die. Instead it lurked in the shadows, growing hungry and strange and mad, fearful of meeting the same fate of its brethren. Perhaps we unknowingly worship it. Perhaps the roads, subways and elevators are its church. Perhaps when we kill each other, we make a sacrifice to it.

I cannot know for sure. All I know is that the "near misses" grew worse and worse until one morning I realized that I couldn't do it anymore. I could not face the thing that lives in traffic. I drove into work at noon on nearly empty streets, and told my partners that I was resigning.

With my reputation, it was not difficult for me to get a job at a good firm in Kitchener (although at a sizable pay cut). My commute was less than half an hour, and not on the 401. I thought if I jigged my schedule just a little, I wouldn't hit any traffic at all.

At first, everything seemed to be working fine. But then I started hitting traffic at odd times, in odd places. Two lane stonedust roads lined by split-rail fencing would be backed up with trucks, cars, motorcycles. And I could see the monster living in the traffic, its hundreds of beady eyes, its tentacles and teeth, squirming and flexing in some horrendous dark pit far outside of this world. People said traffic was getting worse because of the tech boom led by Research In Motion. But I knew what it was. I was cursed.

Pretty soon, no matter when I left home, I was confronted by a tightly-packed mob of cars with the thing staring at me through their taillights and breathing at me through their tailpipes. My accidents were getting more and more serious; I quit my job after I was t-boned making a left hand turn on an advanced green, only to have the ambulance that picked me up get in another accident on the way to the hospital.

I joined a small firm in Guelph. My nerves were shot, and my reputation had taken a serious hit, but I just figured if I could get away from the cursed traffic, I could at least enough to keep up with the mortgage payments. But even sleepy Guelph wasn't safe! I would leave before 6, it was a five minute drive to work in a town of around 100,000 people, but there were taxis, cyclists, jaywalkers. I tried walking to work, but even the sidewalks weren't safe.

So there it is. There is a thing that lives in traffic and it's trying to kill me. That's why I can't go in with you tomorrow. You've got to believe me. Someone has to. You don't know how lonely this is. How ironic that traffic follows me wherever I go, but I always feel so wretchedly alone.

The letter greatly saddened me. Clearly, Andy had been very unwell. If only I'd taken the stupid letter! Instead, I forced him into a situation he couldn't handle, and he panicked so badly that he made his worst fears come true.

And what wretchedly bad luck it was that we ran into such an unaccountable traffic jam on the Hanlon before six! What were the odds of such an improbable occurrence on the specific day I was driving a person with such an unusual phobia into the city! But Andy was right about one thing; traffic is as unpredictable as a tiger. You can never tell when it's going to bite you.

The next morning my commute was particularly bad (it was, I could not help noticing, getting close to the new moon). I could see cars up ahead following too close and changing lanes abruptly and then the taillights started to blink on, and all that red rushed towards me, and the cars slowed, and stopped, as the traffic settled in.

The letter had affected me, and I was a bit nervous. But I turned on an irritating morning show and sent my mind away. I was on my way to work to pay for my wonderful house and care for my loving family. The vagaries of the 401 would take my time, but not my peace of mind, or my sanity.

But at work I found I could not look away from the view outside of my window. I watched the traffic build up at St. Clair and Yonge, and release, over and over again, exactly like the beating of some hideous heart of glowing electric light and burnished metal.

Would Andy's delusions begin to affect me? Would I end up like him? Not if I could do anything about it. I closed the blinds, turned on the music, and put my mind on my work.

Our building is old, and could use more elevators, so at peak times there is often a line. When I was leaving at the end of the day, a big crowd was waiting in the hall. I could tell that I would be lucky to get on the second elevator to arrive. I tried to cram my way forward, and then all of a sudden, I saw it.

I wish I could describe what it was like when the thing popped out at me, but I can't. It was like one of those optical illusions, where a picture could be two women kissing or a glass, and once you see it one way, you can't unsee it. Suddenly the crowd of people was not a crowd at all, but a terrible thing, horribly old and monstrously mad, a hungry elder god that had gone blind from centuries of living in the dark. A kind of dark presence, vague and infinite but somehow distinctly inhuman and horrible and unnatural.

And the moment I saw it, it saw me, and I could feel its anger, and hunger.

Someone shoved me in the back, hard, and I fell forward into the person in front of me. The whole crowd lurched like a mosh pit. I felt my ankle twist, almost snapping. Someone screamed. It was me.

"Who pushed me?" someone shouted from behind.

Eventually, the crowd stabilized and we stood back up. The thing that I had seen was gone, and all the faces looking at me were friendly and solicitous. In spite of this, and my wounded ankle, I did not get in the elevator (the thought of that door closing and trapping me inside was more than I could stand). Instead I limped down the stairs, telling myself the whole way that it was my imagination, that I had seen a good friend die less than a week ago and read a disturbing letter, that all the time in the car was getting to me and that I would be fine. You have never truly been frightened until you have hoped, with all your heart, that you are insane.

When I came out onto the street, I saw the thing in a crowd of people heading down the entrance to the subway, crammed on the streetcars that were rolling past, and in the cars backed up at the stoplights. A horn blared as a car swerved dangerously close to the sidewalk. I fled back inside.

I stood inside leaning on the door in the empty staircase gasping for breath. What was I to do? In the heart of the city at 5:30 p.m. traffic was everywhere. Mount Pleasant? The DVP? Avenue Road? There was nowhere to go. The monster had already eaten me and it was never going to spit me up.

I stayed at work until midnight. On the trip home, traffic was fine on Mount Pleasant and on the 401. I allowed myself to hope that it had all been a kind of vision. But traffic got heavier as I headed west, and there was a jam in Mississauga, right where the 401 went down from 12 lanes to six. It was waiting for me there. All of its red eyes burning. The hot stink of its breath filtering through my vent. The sound of its voice rumbling.

I was rear-ended, twice, but they were just taps. Sweat drenched my clothes, and my heart was beating so hard I thought I might have an attack. I got off the 401, thinking I would beat it on the back-roads but a fatal accident had blocked off Embleton Road, and everything was clogged up, so I pulled a u-turn and fled, even though that was taking me back to the city. I drove too fast, trembling with fear, and I only saw the dump truck backing into the road at the last minute.

By the time the tow truck pulled my car from the ditch, it was three in the morning. Perhaps even the thing had limits of some kind, because the traffic was gone, and I had an easy drive back home.

There was no question of going into work the next day. I was not like a dumb character in a bad horror movie, marching into certain death while the audience hooted. I was a real person, in real life. But by the same token, I could not stay home for ever. As tedious and deadly as traffic is, it is an inescapable fact of life. To refuse to face traffic was to die a slow, beggarly death. It would be better for me, and for my family, to meet my destiny head on. At least if I died on the road my family would get insurance money.

And unlike Andy, I had a rather good idea how to handle the situation. The idea had occurred to me when I was reading his letter, and I was a little surprised that it had not occurred to him.

So after a sleepless morning, I told my wife I was staying in for the day, and when she left for work, and after the babysitter arrived, I set about making the necessary arrangements.

You might expect that it is a difficult thing for a young, urban professional with no connections in the farming community to arrange to kill a cow, but nothing could be further from the truth. Personally killing your food is actually one of the hottest parts of the whole organic and local food movement, (Mark Zuckerberg did it for a year) and Guelph is a great place for that sort of hippie thing. After five minutes of surfing the web I found a place that was able to accommodate me in the afternoon.

I had visions of slitting a cow's throat with an enormous knife, but it was nothing so barbaric. The farmer held the cow, and I pressed a gas powered pistol-like thing to its head, right between its eyes, and pulled the trigger. A shaft of metal jabbed out and penetrated its brains and it dropped to the ground like, well, a dead cow. There was hardly any blood.

The farmer looked at me and asked if I was all right.

"Can you butcher this right now?" I asked.

"It takes about a week," he said.

"I will pay you $5,000 if I walk out of this place with this cow chopped up in two hours," I said.

He raised an eyebrow.

"You can leave the skin on," I added.

The farmer, who struck me as rather unflappable, was clearly shaken. But money talks, and in less than forty five minutes we were loading dismembered cow parts into the back of my car.

I have one of those big green egg barbecues and I stuffed it with charcoal and sprayed it with lighter fluid. Once the flames started to leap up, I cut the beef out of the vacuum-sealed plastic wrapping and laid it on the grill. A pillar of black smoke drifted towards the sky.

The babysitter came outside.

"What are you doing?" she asked.

I thought for a moment, but any lie would have sounded just as crazy as the truth.

"I'm making a burnt offering to the god of traffic," I replied.

The next morning I left deliberately late, at 6:45, so that I hit Guelph Line well after seven. The congestion didn't seem less than usual, but traffic moved along steadily at 90 kph. It was like everyone was content to drive a little slower, to leave a little more space, and stay in their lanes. The voices burbling on the radio were urging people to get out while it lasted.

I got off in Milton and went to a Tim Horton's. There was no line up at the drive through. I sat in my car and sipped a cloying vanilla latte, deliberately tempting things to get worse. Instead, when I got back on the 401 a space opened up next to me so it was easy to merge.

The thing was still all around me, still senile and dangerous, but also sated, drowsy.

When I drove home, things were back to normal. Stop and go. And it was watching me still. I'd hoped I could put things right between us, but I saw this was not the case. It was hungry. And it knew me now. It knew who I was, where I lived. It knew my commute.

So far I've been able to make things work. I guess I've made my peace with it as much as you can make peace with anything so murderous and inhuman. I go in and come home early. If for some reason I absolutely have to be on the road during the dangerous time, I've found a chicken or a duck will do the trick.

After I'm done this writing this confession, I'm going to wave it at the sky and then file it with my lawyer. If anything should happen to me, it'll be released to the public. Maybe that will make it a little more reluctant to crush me. Who knows?

But looking over what I've written, I'm not really sure I see what makes me so special. Sure I saw this big demon, but in practice am I really any different from anyone else on this commute? We all feed it hours of our lives. We all know it could kill us any time. And we just have to build our lives around it, to get along with it any way we can.

4 These things go in cycles

Nigel worked in the bar at the King Edward Hotel. The building was over a hundred years old and the walls were gilded and the furniture was heavy and stuffed to bursting. A bottle of domestic beer was six dollars, plus tax and tip.

Nigel himself was middle-aged and slow-witted, a dumpy balding man in a white shirt with a collar and a bow tie. The only remarkable thing about him was his slight British accent, which went a lot further than, in all fairness, it ought to have done.

One Saturday afternoon, shortly before a large wedding reception was to be held in the dining hall, Nigel was approached by a man who asked for a martini.

"Certainly sir," Nigel said. "How d'you take it?"

"I'll leave it in your capable hands," the man said. He wore an expensive suit and a gold watch flashed from his wrist, but his curly hair stuck out in every direction. Nigel pegged him, accurately as it turned out, as a corporate lawyer. "Just don't give me any of that 'wave the bottle in the direction of Italy' bullshit. If I wanted cold gin, I'd just ask for it."

Nigel could appreciate a connoisseur, although he was not one himself; at home he drank Creemore straight out of the can, usually while watching whatever TSN saw fit to broadcast (even if it was a spelling bee). Because he lacked creativity, he made the martini exactly by the book: filling the shaker with ice, carefully adding the gin and the vermouth in a ratio of four to one, and shaking, slowly and purposefully, for roughly fifteen seconds. Then he poured it into a glass. Finally, he carefully trimmed the usual slice of lemon peel, squeezed out its oil over the drink, and twisted it into a spiral before dropping it in.

The lawyer took one sip and shuddered.

"Perfect," he said. "Thank you."

"My pleasure sir," Nigel said.

"No, thank you," the lawyer said. He put down a twenty on the bar. "Keep the change."

"That's very generous of you, sir," Nigel said.

"Do you know how hard it is to find a decent martini in this city?" the lawyer said. "First of all, no one knows what a martini is. Butterscotch schnapps? Vanilla vodka? Goldschlager? You do not put any of these things in a martini! A martini is made of gin and vermouth. I will grant you vodka. That's how fair I am. I won't make you call it a vodka martini. But that is the limit."

"I don't like sweet drinks myself, sir," Nigel said.

"Then," the lawyer continued, "on the other end of the spectrum, you have all this macho bullshit. I blame Hemingway. He started all this 'I'm-too-tough-for-Vermouth baloney.' You know the LCBO put out a classic cocktail brochure, and it said to put one or two drops of vermouth in a gin martini? One or two drops?"

"IBA stipulates a four to one ratio, sir," Nigel remarked.

"Exactly," the lawyer said. "You know, I grew up in a Jewish household. My father didn't drink martinis. I didn't drink them at school. I had no exposure until I started articling. My articling principal would give me what he called martinis. Straight gin! I had to pretend to like them! I thought I hated martinis! Finally, one day, we're in New York City, my wife and I, we're out with her friends. I say I don't like martinis, but they ordered me one anyway, and blammo!"

The lawyer threw his hands up in the air.

"No wait," the lawyer said. "Not blammo with an exclamation mark. It was a mellow blammo. E.B. White called the martini the 'elixir of quietude.' That's what it was like. All these things people had written about the martini, and I just never got it, I never really saw it. But it's the perfect before dinner cocktail. All of those weird flavors come to make something greater than the sum of its parts. Cold and clear and good. Eloquent. A hell of a drink."

"A classic," Nigel said.

The lawyer drank more of the martini.

"I gotta go to this wedding," he complained. "It's my partner's daughter."

"My condolences, sir," Nigel said.

"Give me another," the lawyer said. "With an olive, this time."

While Nigel was shaking the shaker, the lawyer looked around the bar, taking it all in: the furniture, the stolid bartender, the drink, and he said, with conviction: "Somebody should open a martini bar in this city. I mean a real martini bar, with real martinis."

"Yes," Nigel said. "They should, shouldn't they?"

A week later the lawyer came back into the bar.

"I'm going to open my own restaurant," he said. "And I want you to work for me."

Nigel was rather shocked, but his placid countenance (he bore a striking resemblance to Mr. Potato-Head) did not register any emotion. The lawyer mistook his confusion for Zen-like serenity, and pressed on.

"I already signed the lease," the lawyer said. "It's on Temperance, just north of First Canadian Place. We open our doors in three months. I'm going to make you an offer you can't refuse."

"All right sir," Nigel said. "Shall I make you a drink?"

Nigel was in the hotel workers' union, and he had benefits, plus a pension to look forward to, but it was indeed an offer he could not refuse. The lawyer (whose name was Brad Lewis) gave him a 30 per cent raise and five per cent of the business.

And so, despite some serious misgivings of the too-good-to-be-true variety, a few months later Nigel found himself standing in a newly renovated bar in the heart of Toronto's financial district. Everything was sleek and minimalist, not so much modern as timeless. Behind the bar hung a sign that read: A MARTINI ALWAYS INCLUDES GIN AND VERMOUTH, BUT WE WILL MAKE YOU ANY KIND OF DRINK YOU LIKE. IF YOU WANT COLD GIN, JUST ASK.

The bar itself was made of dark granite. It was far enough away from the back wall for an entire team of men to move around, and given the level of complexity to which Mr. Lewis was intent on raising the martini, an entire team was necessary. There was a special freezer to hold the glasses and shakers, an apprentice bartender who had been hired to do no more than prepare the garnishes, and two men who were to double as dishwashers and bouncers. All of them looked to Nigel to teach them the perfect way to make a martini.

Fortunately, by this point, Nigel had done plenty of research on the Internet. Not that it was necessary, since simply describing the process of making a martini mandated by the IBA impressed everyone, as long as it was delivered in a sufficiently haughty tone of voice.

Nigel had to admit that the whole complicated operation behind the bar was fairly impressive once it was all set up. It looked good; clean and simple, like a hallmark back to a golden era. And who was to say that he was not onto something? Crantinis and Cosmopolitans were waning in popularity, while cocktails that Don Draper drank were waxing. Nigel began to allow himself a little hope.

The opening was wildly successful. Brad was a social fellow with twenty years worth of contacts downtown, and just about everyone showed up. A DJ got the evening started off, eventually giving way to a four-piece jazz band. The place was rammed, warm, loud. Everyone slopped gin all over each other trying to drink out of the frustratingly impractical martini glasses. Finally Brad, very drunk, got up to make a speech.

"I won't say this bar is like it was in the old days," Brad said. "The reality is we live in a world where they sell you rum and coke in a can, and margarita mix, and jagr bombs. A place like this is self-conscious. You can never really go back to the old days. Still, do we really want to go back to the old days? I don't think so. We're more like those immigrants that go on and on about the old country, but we don't really want to move back there, we want to stay in our nice suburb in Woodbridge. And why shouldn't we? For all our griping and moaning, we live in the best of all possible worlds, where you can go a little west of here and drink vanilla vodka or stay here and get a real martini. To the best of all possible worlds!"

And everyone laughed and cheered, but not Nigel, for by this time he was taking the martini very seriously indeed. His hands were wet and cold, so that his fingers had gone greenish-white. The pungent aroma of gin, like pine needles, had penetrated the deepest reaches of his sinuses. And he was rich. The martinis were being sold for eight dollars each and since everyone was running a tab, tips were likely to average over 15 per cent.

'The Elixir of Quietude' (as it was called) remained popular after opening day. Happy hour was from four thirty to seven. Brad managed to hire university students to play live jazz every night of the week, and so they got a decent after dinner crowd for the financial district. It was a different kind of place, in its strictness, its fastidious and singular devotion, and its timelessness.

It was the best year of Nigel's life. Opening up at eleven to catch the lunch rush. The drinkers in the afternoon, sometimes by themselves, reading a book or watching TV or wanting to chat, sometimes in small groups, loud and boisterous in the almost empty bar. The happy hour crowd in their suits, the men with loosened ties, the women leaving lipstick on their glasses. And then the party crowd late at night, with their short skirts and tight shiny shirts and the jazz wailing in the background, and one martini after another, stirred or shaken, hands numb with the divine cold, the clear drink in the frosted glass, a little shimmer of icy water forming on the surface, the olives in odd numbers. He worked eleven hours a day, six days a week, with no vacation. But he didn't even feel the time going by. It was like a dream.

But then the year passed and Nigel, as a five per cent owner, inquired regarding his share of the profits. Brad informed him there were none.

That night Nigel went to bed with a dark worm of suspicion burrowing into his heart. Was Brad stealing from him? Too-good-to-be-true was rearing its ugly head. He was unable to prevent certain dark, ungrateful, anti-Jewish thoughts from swimming just beneath the surface of his mind.

The next day one of his afternoon regulars, a lawyer named Eddy Faskin, came in at 3 pm to order a martini and read 'The Economist'. Nigel discretely asked him for some advice.

"If you're a shareholder, ask for all the financial information," Eddy said. "I'll come in tomorrow and look it over for you if you let me drink for free."

Nigel was so anxious (perhaps it was a mistake, perhaps it could be worked out) that he e-mailed Brad from his new iPhone that very moment. The e-mail was, in inverse proportion to Nigel's disquiet, scrupulously polite. By seven that night, Brad had e-mailed him back, attaching all the financials as a pdf.

"Should have sent this to you earlier," Brad wrote. "Sorry! Work's been nuts."

The next day, Nigel set a perfect martini on a cocktail napkin in front of Eddy. Eddy tasted it, held the glass up to the light, and licked his lips.

"I never even liked martinis before I came here," Eddy said.

Then he spent ten minutes scrolling through the documents on his laptop before he shut it and smiled at Nigel.

"This bar lost five grand last year," Eddy said.

Nigel did not say anything, but despite his normal lack of expression, something about his bearing must have communicated skepticism.

"Don't believe me?" Eddy said.

"Well sir," Nigel said. "We're just always so busy."

"Well Brad's a shitty businessman," Eddy said, and quaffed deeply before continuing. "He's overpaying all the staff by 20 to 30 per cent. The renovations were super expensive. He didn't sign a personal guarantee, which was maybe his one smart move, but it means he's paying a high rate of interest on his loan. But most of all, the rent is too fucking high. Do you know how much he's paying for this dinky little space?"

Nigel, of course, did not.

"Six grand a month," Eddy said, and shook his head. "Jesus. You tell me how a business is supposed to operate under those conditions."

Nigel was crushed.

"I suppose he will shut the business down," Nigel said. "If we didn't make money this year, I don't know how we ever could."

"Oh, I wouldn't worry about that," Eddy said. "You know Brad makes close to a million dollars a year, right? He's a dynamo for his firm. Real workhorse. $5,000 a year is nothing for him to have the fun of owning a place like this. Hell, he probably got $5,000 of work referred to him just from meeting people in here. Not to mention he can set the losses against what he earns from his real job."

"So you think he will keep it open?"

"Well, sure, for a while," Eddy said. "But not forever. Just make sure you're saving your money."

In addition to his iPhone, Nigel had acquired a new car and a house in the Beaches whose mortgage payments could justly be described as elephantine. He was sorely tempted to pour out a martini for himself, but restrained himself.

Eddy, a small, hard, cynical-looking man with very little hair, one of those quiet men who really open up when you get to know them, said:

"Do you ever wonder why the rent for a place like this is so high that you can't run a business here? I mean, how does it keep up?"

"Haven't a clue," Nigel said.

"Because everyone wants to own a martini bar," Eddy said. "Here's Brad Lewis, he makes a million a year, but he wants to own a bar, something he really has no idea how to do. And there are so many guys like him running around that they drive the rent up so high no one can actually run a real business here. Each one of these places lasts until someone gets bored, and then when the party's over, someone else just steps in and takes his place. It's like an epidemic of daydreaming."

"If you say so, sir," Nigel said.

Eddy took another sip from his glass.

"The real money in the gold rush," Eddy said, "was selling pickaxes."

A month later, Brad came into the bar at ten thirty in the morning while Nigel was opening up. The moment Nigel saw him he knew there would be bad news.

"I'll have a martini," Brad said. "Make it just like you did for me the first time, only a double."

Heart pounding, but outwardly calm, Nigel did as he was instructed. The moment after the little twist of lemon peel hit the surface of the drink, Brad spoke.

"I'm getting divorced."

His face twisted into an expression of exaggerated grief, like a sad clown.

"My wife is leaving me for a librarian!" Brad said, his voice breaking. "Not even her personal trainer or anything dignified like that. He's fifteen years younger than her, but she says he understands her! The librarian! I should have known. She was in there taking books out every day."

"I'm terribly sorry sir," Nigel said.

Brad drank.

"It's all very amiable," he said, with profound bitterness. "The kids are at university. I'll keep taking care of their tuition. She'll get the house, and I won't really have to pay much support. I guess they'll live off of the librarian's salary."

"Where will you go, sir?"

"I'll have to move in with my girlfriend," Brad groaned.

Nigel hesitated a beat, and then said: "Sorry sir?"

"The yoga instructor," Brad said, groaning (if possible) even harder. "Yoga! I hate yoga. It's like the opposite of a martini. Have you ever had this tea they make? With the leaves just floating around in the cup, like water in a gutter? Can you please tell me what these people have against tea bags?"

Nigel's eyes narrowed. His mind was, you might charitably say, 'racing.' Racing like a very fat man frantically pedaling on a too-small tricycle, but falling further and further behind a slow-moving ice cream truck.

"If you don't need to pay support, perhaps you can keep the bar," Nigel said.

"No, no," Brad said. "We tried to make the numbers work. The problem is that the assets are worth more than the business as a going concern. The lawyers shat themselves sideways when they saw the financials. This space is going to get turned into a Starbucks."

Nigel poured himself a martini, which would have met Ernest Hemingway's approval.

"A Starbucks! There's like three of them across the street! Some people are just terrible businessmen." Brad shook his head and looked around. "Boy, I am really going to miss this place."

"Me too, sir," Nigel said.

Brad sighed.

"I had it all. Hubris! That was my problem. Man isn't meant to have it all. Oh well. These things go in cycles. We'll end up back on top again, you and me."

Of this, Nigel was uncertain. There was no job for him back at the King Eddy, where everything was based on seniority. He had assumed a reckless amount of debt based on his salary, and now he was going to have to compete for jobs with buxom blonde twenty-one year olds who would work for less than minimum wage and tips.

Anyway, they had a hell of a closing party. By invite only, and the place was jammed so tight no one could move. It was hard to believe something that looked so good, so successful, something that looked just like money, could be hollow, nothing but a big vanity project.

Brad passed out in the washroom, nearly drowning himself in a toilet full of vomit. The saddest moment for Nigel came at the end of the night when the other employees paid their respect to him as their chief. None of them had ever once questioned Nigel's status as an expert in a cocktail that only had two ingredients. It was like they had all been in on the joke.

The last man to leave was the fellow who specialized in trimming the lemon peel. His name was Barry, and he was young, East Indian, and borderline mentally retarded. Never again, Nigel thought, would Barry wear a suit to work, converse as an equal with millionaires, or be considered an expert at anything. Maudlin, and slightly drunk, Nigel speculated that Barry would get hooked on crack and become a male prostitute. When their eyes met Nigel was almost brought to tears. For Barry's sake, he restrained himself.

Outside, he looked at the dark windows, the polished metal of the barstools, the commanding sign behind the bar, and the name of the restaurant writ in neon: The Elixir of Quietude. And then he lowered his head and marched to the subway stop, like a soldier who had surrendered to a hated enemy after a lengthy siege.

Not two days later, Nigel was sitting on his lay-z-boy in front of his newly purchased big screen television with a can of Creemore in his hand. He had canceled his cable service and so he was watching Fawlty Towers on DVD. His iPhone rang.

"Hello."

"Is this Nigel?"

"Yes."

"Nigel, it's me, Randy Hawkins."

"..."

"You remember me?"

"I think ..."

"We met at the bar, remember? I'm a friend of Brad's. We talked about port."

"Oh, yes sir," Nigel said. This was a lie. Men often remembered conversations with Nigel, but Nigel rarely remembered the conversations he had with them, any more than a parrot in a pet shop remembered the words it repeated to the capering children outside.

"Anyway, I know you're not strictly a martini guy, and I know you know a lot about port. Are you into other fortified wines? Like brandy, and sherry?"

"And cognac, sir?"

"Yes, and cognac, but mostly port and sherry, is what I'm interested in."

"Of course sir," Nigel said. "I'm certified by the IBA. And my old dad used to have a glass of sherry after dinner every night."

"That's what I'm talking about!" Randy bellowed. Nigel remembered him now. Big guy, slicked back blond hair, very red face. Blue collar businessman who owned a string of car-washes. Expensive sports jacket and a crisp dress shirt with just one button too many undone. "You know no one drinks sherry anymore? I went to visit the Glenfiddich distillery when I was playing golf in Scotland, you know what they said? They told us to drink more sherry, because there aren't enough sherry casks to age the Scotch in! Sherry is a great drink."

"Illustrious history, sir."

"Now Brad's place was great," Randy said, "but I think the whole Mad-Men-classic-cocktails thing is a bit overdone. You look around this city, you've got a million wine bars, a million beer bistros, a million scotch bars, do you have even one quality restaurant and bar, maybe some place with a little music, that specializes in fortified wines?"

"I can't think of a single one sir," Nigel said.

"Nigel," Randy trumpeted, "I am going to start that restaurant. I just signed a five year lease up at Yonge and Eglinton. I'd like you to be the night bartender."

Brad was at the launch party. It was so crowded that it was a simple matter for Nigel to mix him a quick martini, on the house, without attracting the attention of the yoga instructor.

5 Know its name

Alligators and crocodiles hunt the same way. They paddle around the surface of the water, their bodies as still as logs, their reptilian eyes (the pupils dark vertical slits set in amber) just barely poking out into the air. They submerge at the first sound and wait for their prey to approach the water, in which they are completely invisible in depths of less than a foot.

The attack takes place in less than a second, and once their jaws close shut, on an arm or a leg or any part of the body, they never let go. Instead they roll wildly, trying to rip off a limb or break the spine, or they dig in with their small, clawed feet and try to drag their catch under the water to drown.

Despite these similarities there is one crucial difference between alligators and crocodiles. Alligators do not see humans as food, and crocodiles do. When an alligator hears a human approach, it will flee. A crocodile, on the other hand, will go on the hunt.

It is this difference in temperament, which distinguishes truly dangerous animals from merely threatening ones. The decision to incorporate humanity into the secret world of animals, of predator and prey, instead of treating us as outsiders. That they see us and know us and that they are not afraid.

Keystone Heights is about 45 minutes east of Gainesville. The country is dotted with freshwater lakes and green trees whose branches are heavy with moss. The air feels like it bears a heavy burden too, of heat and water, perhaps of something else. The ground is soft and swampy and the grass grows high. Bugs hum in the air, hovering, waiting to feed.

The houses downtown are clean and spacious, with orderly yards. In the outskirts they grow smaller, plainer, shabbier, and wilder, with ferns and trees and moss and secrets. Many are marked with foreclosure signs and abandoned.

Gavin Rollins sat at the bar in Flannigan's and drank his coke slowly, so as to make it last. He was watching the television above the bar with a tense expression, a kind of bracing, like a man who has nothing more to hope for than a reprieve and does not expect to receive even that.

The television was showing a fight from the undercard of the evening's UFC pay-per-view event. This match was between Joshua Parker, a lanky 205 pounder with a pink Mohawk and the wings of an angel tattooed on his back, and Rafael Silva, a squat Brazilian with a shaved head and look of calculating Third World amorality in his eyes.

Silva was a Muai Thai brawler with little-to-no wrestling ability and he was coming off two straight unanimous decision losses. Parker was a former Division I wrestler and the fight was essentially a gift. But he wasn't going to win. Gavin could tell. It was in the way he circled, afraid, glancing over at his corner. And it was in the way Silva plodded forward, his fists high and close to his face, his head weaving back and forth. Coming on as smooth and casual as a gator that sees a dog at the water's edge taking a drink.

"You stupid asshole," Gavin said.

Parker (who was meekly circling backwards around the cage) attempted a superman punch. He telegraphed it so badly that it worked to his advantage; Silva countered hard enough to kill an ox, but wildly. The punch whistled past Parker's head and he danced away again.

"Oh, you cock-sucker," Gavin said.

"Hey," Doreen said. "Watch your language, Gavin."

Gavin looked at her. He resembled a hobgoblin with his bald head and his ears that jutted out perpendicular from his skull. Nose smashed flat a thousand times. Teeth too white and straight and uniform to be real. Scar tissue flowering around eyes that looked both threatened and dangerous. A man who was quick to take offense and act. But something softened in him and he looked back at the television.

Parker was still dancing the edge of the cage. He was afraid. Silva knew it and so did the audience (who was booing) and so did Joe Rogan (who was screeching for Parker to "hit him – hit him!") and so did Gavin. Gavin knew it best of all because he'd felt the same fear himself, two years ago, when he'd fought Parker in a "Real Fighting Championship" event in front of maybe 250 heckling "fans."

The fight on TV ended, predictably, when Parker finally went in for the takedown. Silva caught him in the temple with a knee. Parker's mouth-guard went flying and he flopped onto his back and lay on the ground as pale and as boneless as a fish in the bottom of a boat. Silva didn't even hit him again; he just turned and raised his hands to the howling crowd.

"It's all over!" Goldberg screamed.

Gavin almost swore again. Instead he gritted his teeth and his eyes bulged out of his head and his hand tightened so hard on his cup it would have shattered if it had not been plastic.

"You take it easy Gavin," Doreen said. She was tall with orange hair and looked vaguely like a pretty woman who had melted.

"Give me a beer," Gavin said.

She clucked her tongue. "Not likely."

"You've got to serve me," Gavin said.

"I sure as hell don't."

"You don't have any right not to serve me."

"Why don't you just calm down, honey? You'd think that you'd be happy he lost, the way he kicked the shit out of you."

"He's a jackass anyway," someone called from further down the bar. "Of all the pricks that were on the show, he was by far the worst. Had it coming."

"He jacked off into that Jamaican's dude's protein shake," someone else said.

"I'd have fucking killed him," the first voice said.

Gavin looked at the drink in his hand. Studied it. Then he drank what remained in the glass and set it down and stood up.

"Gavin," Doreen said. "Why don't you stay and watch the rest of the fights? You don't have to buy anything."

"No," he said.

"You know I can't let you have a drink."

"I know. I appreciate that."

"Where are you going?"

"It's private."

"You aren't going to get into trouble? Where are you going at this hour?"

"I'm going to a meeting," he said.

"Oh, well, I'm sorry."

"Never mind."

"I didn't mean to pry."

"Forget it."

"Have a good time."

"You too," Gavin said.

He walked out into the warm night rain and tugged his jacket around his neck. He thought of Parker two years ago, shooting in with all the skill and confidence you could get from five years at the University of Florida. When Gavin got on the highway he headed west to the Baptist church. His shoes squelched into the mud as he stepped over wax cups from McDonald's and Snickers wrappers. The tall grass whispered in the rain.

As was usual with him at times like these, with the bland road stretching out empty in front of him, he felt a creeping despair rising in his heart.

Suddenly he was caught in the headlights of an approaching car and he squinted, which turned his ugly face into something that would not have been out of place had it been carved in stone on a cathedral. The car made a screaming noise as it skidded to a stop.

Gavin was blinded by the light. He heard the door open and then he heard her call his name and suddenly she was silhouetted against the blaze of the headlights, like an angel coming down from heaven with its back to the sun.

She said his name again.

"Kristy?" he said.

"Oh my god," she said, and ran into his arms. When she got closer he could see her better. She was still beautiful. Older, not unchanged superficially, but the same somehow.

He caught her and held her and he was so surprised he couldn't think of a thing to say.

"Thank god it's you!" she said.

"Kristy," he said. The surprise was so big and powerful it crowded out anything else; nerves, joy, sexual arousal.

She pulled away from him and he felt a sudden moment of loss; it was only then that he'd realized how good it had felt to have her in his arms.

"We have to go," she said, running back to her car. "Come on! Hurry!"

Gavin glanced around him, as if there was something in the swampy wasteland that he might forget to bring along. Then he shook his head and got in the car. Before he could close the door the car was already screeching forward and to the left in the first leg of a three-point turn.

"Whoa, whoa, what's the matter? What's the matter?"

"It's my brother."

"Todd?"

"They've got my brother." She turned her face to him and he saw that tears had given her mascara raccoon eyes. "We've got to get over there right now."

"Well, okay," Gavin said. "All right. Who's got him?"

"Bendis," she said, and Gavin felt an icy hand clench in the bottom of his stomach.

"Bendis?" he said.

"Fucking Bendis."

"What does Bendis want with Todd?"

"Todd owes him money."

Gavin let this sink in for a moment. They were ripping down the highway at eighty miles an hour.

"Bendis lent your brother money?"

"Todd ... Todd's in a lot of trouble. He was really unhappy."

Getting in debt to someone like Bendis was not exactly the kind of trouble Todd usually got into. Todd was stupid enough to do it, but Gavin couldn't understand why an ordinarily pretty together member of the Hell's Angels like Alan Bendis would loan money to a fuck-up like Todd Marvin.

"Can you tell me the story from the beginning?" Gavin said.

Kristy suddenly jammed on the brakes and turned right onto a gravel road heading down into the swamp towards the lake. They were heading, Gavin realized, towards the clubhouse. The icy hand in his stomach clenched just a little tighter and he felt his mouth grow dry.

"He owes them money, I don't know why, I brought him out here to talk to them, he said it would just be a minute, and then they grabbed him and I had to run back to the car and I just drove for it, I just needed to find someone."

She looked at him again through her bleary eyes. Her hair was brown with just a touch of red, her eyes were light green, her features were intelligent and fine (some, not Gavin, might describe them as sharp), and freckles were lightly spread across her face.

"Should we call the cops?" Gavin said.

"We can't call the cops on Todd," she said. "He's been in a lot of trouble. He's on parole. We haven't even paid the lawyer from last time."

The road plunged down. It was covered with grass and moss and as spongy as a dog's tongue. The tall grass rose up on either side of the road and the trees spread their heavy branches overhead. They turned a corner and Gavin saw the clubhouse, peeling and faded and leaning a little bit over the murky water. Three big Harleys were parked out front.

This is really happening, Gavin thought, *and I'm going to die*.

But then he thought of the road stretching out and leading to nowhere, and he hopped out of the car without hesitation when it skidded to a stop.

"Get the car turned around," Gavin said. "We're going to have to go in a hurry."

The clubhouse door was bolted from the inside and Gavin, without thinking too much, put his shoulder to it. The bolt snapped off and the door flew open and he came inside and, for a moment, froze in his tracks.

The clubhouse consisted of one rectangular room. Plastic tables and chairs were scattered around and a kitchenette was in one corner. A big wire-framed fan was set up in the window and beer bottles were scattered all over the floor.

A silent, deathly serious struggle was taking place. No one made any noise except for the occasionally grunt of exertion or gasp for air. Two bikers, burly fellows in stained t-shirts with wild beards and stars-and-stripes bandanas, were holding Todd on the ground. A third was standing over them, holding something in his hands wrapped in a heavy piece of plastic tarp. Whatever it was, it was wriggling.

"Undo his pants," the standing biker said. Gavin could tell from his voice (deep as a gravel pit) and from his greying red hair that it was Alan Bendis.

"No!" Todd screamed. "No don't!"

One of the bikers sat on Todd's feet and reached for his fly.

"No! No! Don't!"

Todd's voice was high and reedy, like a little girl.

"I'll get you the money!"

Gavin came up behind them and punched Bendis as hard as he could in the back of the head. Bendis made a strangely inquisitive noise (blark?) and stumbled to his knees and dropped his squirming bundle. A baby alligator slithered out and sprang forward and bit one of the bikers holding Todd on the arm.

"Motherfucker!" the biker shouted and stood up and shook his arm back and forth.

The other biker was still sitting on Todd's legs and unzipping his fly and looking at Gavin with a surprised expression on his face. Gavin kicked hard and short and compact, Muai Thai style, and smacked his shin into the biker's temple. Then he reached down, grabbed Todd by the shoulder and jerked him loose from the pile. Todd's pants came off.

"Run!" Gavin barked. "Fucking run!"

Without looking to see if Todd was following, Gavin bolted for the front door. After a moment the bikers started to bellow in rage and Gavin could literally feel their thunderous footfalls reverberating through the cheap linoleum.

Gavin ran out into the muggy swamp air. The car was waiting; Kristy had even opened the back door on the driver's side. Gavin jumped in and he was followed a moment later by Todd, wearing only a Nine Inch Nails t-shirt and his tighty-whiteys. One of the bikers came out the front door as Kristy floored it. The alligator was still hanging from his arm like a bizarre charm bracelet.

In an instant they were gone.

Todd put his hands to his face and screamed and screamed. Gavin had to reach across him to pull the door shut.

"Oh my god! Oh my god!"

"Shh," Kristy said. "Shh, it's okay Todd, we got you."

"Oh my god," Todd wailed, and started to cry, messily. Snot came out of his nose, and he shouted suddenly, almost petulantly: "They were trying to kill me! Oh my god."

Gavin leaned his head against the window and closed his eyes.

They headed west into town. Todd cried, kicked, and periodically screamed. Hyperventilated, even, for a little while. Kristy kept looking back at him and telling him to calm down. She didn't look at Gavin at all.

Eventually Todd started to calm down, just made little dramatic gasping noises. Then he put his head in his hands and started to shake. He said: "What am I going to do? Those guys are fucking psychos. I'm fucked. I'm fucked. I hate this town! You should have just let them kill me."

At this point Gavin caught Kristy's gaze in the rear view mirror and he could see the agony and the embarrassment and the love written there.

"You'd better slow down," Gavin said. "You might as well go the speed limit now."

"They might follow us," Kristy said.

"It's a small town," Gavin said. "They know where we live."

Kristy and Todd were upstairs talking with their father. Every now and then their voices would rise in anger, Todd's high and complaining, Mr. Marvin bellowing like a bull, Kristy exasperated and pleading.

Gavin waited on the sofa with his hands on his knees and stared at the dark television. Eventually Kristy came downstairs.

"I can go if you want," Gavin said.

"Don't be ridiculous," Kristy said. "Just hang on for a second. My dad and my brother are just ... you know how it is."

"I missed you," Gavin said.

Kristy looked away and smiled, a little. "It's good to see you too, Gavin," she said.

There was a sudden shout from upstairs and Kristy ran back up the stairs.

A moment later Mr. Marvin stomped downstairs. He fixed his eyes on Gavin, who straightened his back a little.

"You want a drink?" Marvin said.

"I'll take a Coke if you've got one."

"Do you want a beer?"

"No, thank you sir."

"You gave it up, is what Kristy said."

"Yes sir, I did."

"How long ago?"

"Fourteen months."

Marvin grunted. He was short, with a grey crew cut and a large, hard beer gut that hung over the elastic waistband of his sweatpants. For a moment he disappeared into the kitchen and then he came out with two glass bottles of Pepsi.

"Thank you," Gavin said.

Marvin sat down heavily in the Lay-Z-Boy and pulled the handle that raised the footrest. He looked over at Gavin.

"I suppose I should thank you for saving my son."

Gavin shrugged.

Marvin shook his head and clenched his jaw. "Boy never could do right. At least Kristy turned out. Although she gave me plenty to worry about in her time, too."

Marvin looked at Gavin and the meaning was plain. All Gavin said was:

"Well, maybe there's hope for Todd yet, then."

Marvin grunted sceptically.

"People can change," Gavin said.

"No," Marvin said. "Not really, not deep down, they can't."

He looked at Gavin again.

"You never had a prayer with my daughter."

Gavin looked down. He was surprised when Marvin spoke again, quickly.

"Hell son. I didn't mean it like that. I didn't mean to put you down there, it's just my way. What I meant was, I meant it like, you don't need to regret. You understand? You strike me as a man that's carrying quite a load. In your heart. It can't be easy to have been such a son of a bitch. You get to thinking if only you'd done things differently, things would have gone differently. If you follow me. But you shouldn't do that. It wasn't ever going to work with you and Kristy. What were you anyway, a cage fighter?"

"Yeah."

"That stuff that's on the TV all the time?"

"Yeah."

"Jesus," Marvin said, and wiped the back of his neck. "All I meant was you don't need to beat yourself up over something you did or you didn't do. It ain't about anything like that. You need to let that go, all that go. You're young and you've got your future ahead of you. You can't think about the past."

"Okay," Gavin said.

"I didn't mean to put you down there."

"I getcha," Gavin said.

"Hell, take a run at her if you'd like. Least you aren't a Democrat, like that smart-mouth she's running with now."

Gavin favoured the old man with a smile, quick and small and genuine, there for a moment, now gone.

Marvin took a drink of Pepsi.

"I wouldn't bother if I was you," Marvin said. "But something tells me you aren't going to listen to me."

He turned the TV on and they watched the news in silence until Kristy came downstairs.

"I really appreciate it," Kristy said. "I don't know what I would have done without you. He might have died."

They were in the car now, driving to an apartment building not far from the trailer park where Gavin actually lived.

"That's okay," Gavin said.

"You risked your life."

"No, not really."

"Yes you did."

Gavin shrugged.

"Todd never had it easy. You know what my dad's like. And Todd, well, Todd was always pretty different. It was how God made him. He couldn't be any other way. They sent him to one of those camps when he was a teenager. A Christian change ministry. Something bad happened to him there. I don't know what it was, but he won't talk about it. He tried to kill himself. The scars are all over his arms. Dad keeps talking about sending him back. He keeps saying that Todd'd be happier if he was normal. I'm sure he would be much happier if he was normal. Only, he can't just be normal."

Gavin thought of his own, dim memories of his father. Stomping work boots and a slashing belt that disappeared around the time he turned five. He'd always thought that kind of thing made you tougher. As a child and a young man he'd bragged about the beatings he'd taken from people who'd been responsible for him and he'd always had nothing but contempt for kids like Todd.

These feelings still rose in him faithfully, same old response to the same old stimuli. But he'd learned to distrust them, to wonder if all the kicks and bruises he'd taken had really made him stronger, just pushed the weakness down, hidden it. That's what they said in the meetings, sometimes. Gavin didn't know if he believed it but he did know he couldn't trust his instincts any more. They'd brought him to some bad places. Now he was unsure about his every step.

Like now, for instance.

He couldn't take his eyes off her face. And he thought: what to say? How was he supposed to handle this? His first instinct was just to lay it out there. But he knew that wouldn't work. The old man was right. Or was he? These days his confidence was gone. And if he couldn't trust himself, how could he do anything?

She glanced over at him and looked away, smiled, a little embarrassed.

"Everyone has to carry their own water, Kristy," he said. "It isn't always fair. But it is what it is."

They drove in silence the rest of the way. The car stopped in front of the apartment building and Gavin opened the door.

"It was good to see you again Gavin."

"You too."

He stepped out and she said his name. He looked back.

"Can you do me a favour?"

"Sure," Gavin said.

"I have to go back to Tallahassee," she said. "Can you just check in on him? See if he's doing all right?"

Gavin smiled.

"Okay," he said. "I'm not sure he'll really want to see me."

Kristy rolled her eyes.

"Who cares what he thinks. Please, just make sure he's okay."

"All right," Gavin said. "Have a good night, Kristy."

"Bye," she said.

He shut the door and she drove off, leaving him alone in the late night rain. The small apartment complex crouched over him. There were no stars in the sky. Gavin walked back to the road and turned north and headed into the darkness that led to the trailer park.

His key was just rattling into the lock of the door to his trailer when he felt the presence behind him.

"Hey Gavin," the deep and pitiless voice said. "How you doing?"

Gavin put his keys back in his pocket and turned around.

Bendis gave Gavin one of those little black biker helmets with an iron cross painted on the side and he rode on the back of the Harley with his arms wrapped around Bendis' thick, leather-bound chest. The smell of armpits and cigarettes was overwhelming. Bikers buzzed ahead of them and behind, a rumbling line of thunder.

When they arrived at the clubhouse two men came outside, carrying cans of Old Milwaukee with one hand and grabbing their crotches with the other. One of them had a nasty black eye. The other's forearm was bandaged.

Everyone parked their bikes and stood up. In total there were about a dozen. They weren't all tall but they were all big, hefty motherfuckers. Beards, tattooed arms, hanging guts. They weren't going to win many footraces but if they got a hold of you, you wouldn't be going anywhere.

Bendis took his helmet off and brushed the hair away from his eyes.

"Didn't think they let you throw rabbit punches even in MMA," Bendis said.

Gavin said nothing.

"I'm more of a boxing man, myself," Bendis said. "All that rolling around on the mat's for queers. You queer too, Gavin?"

"No."

"You sure?" Bendis said. "Risking your life, to save your boyfriend? What was that is all about? Love?"

"Jesus Bendis, you're the one that gave him money. How much did you give him anyway?"

"Two hundred thousand dollars," Bendis said.

It took only a moment to realize that Bendis wasn't joking; the hushed, almost embarrassed silence of the bikers told Gavin all he needed to know. Bendis was smiling a little. Gavin almost felt his heart stop.

"Two ..." he started, than trailed off.

"Two hundred large," Bendis said. "Into that fuck."

"Well," Gavin said, then cleared his throat. "Well a fool and his money are soon fucking parted, Alan."

Bendis laughed.

"Come for a ride with me," he said.

"I just did."

"I mean on our boat."

Inside the clubhouse a number of rather worn-out looking women were lounging in the kitchenette smoking cigarettes. Their bleary and broken eyes tracked Gavin to the back door where the airboat was waiting. Gavin slid open the screen door and stepped out onto its gently rocking surface. Bendis followed, and then the biker with the black eye. The boat noticeably sunk.

"You know anything about alligators, Gavin?" Bendis said.

When you couldn't stop someone from fucking you, Gavin believed, you shouldn't do anything at all. Whatever you did would just give them satisfaction, a little piece of you.

The biker with the black eye started the boat's fan and the rush of fake wind pattered the surface of the water down. They drifted away from the clubhouse.

"Alligators are scared of people," Bendis said. "Oh, not the little ones, the babies. They don't have no fear of people, so they'll bite. But they're small. Now the big ones, they hear a man coming, they slide under the water and skedaddle. Unless they lose their fear of people too."

When they got away from the shore, pushing through the tall grass and the waving reeds and the clinging lily pads, the fan fired up suddenly and they leapt out across the water.

"That's why you're not supposed to feed the gators," Bendis shouted over the fan. He smiled and brushed his greying reddish (almost orange) hair away from his eyes.

A fine mist hung in the air around them. The biker steered the boat by pushing a pole back and forth that turned the fan.

"You feed the gators and they lose their fear of people," Bendis shouted. "It's funny how their minds work, or don't work, I guess. They don't get grateful. They don't get tame. They just stop getting scared. That's why it's important to keep things scared of you. You understand? Do you understand me?"

Gavin didn't move.

Bendis' face changed subtly.

It was time to nod. Gavin nodded.

Bendis' face changed back. He smiled and reached under the seat and pulled out a cooler that was stained orange around its lid.

The fan ramped back down again and they skimmed over the water to the other side of the little lake. No houses or roads were on that side. Just the tall trees and ferns by the bank and the reeds and grass coming out of the water. There was a rustling noise and then heavy splashes as the gators slithered down into the water.

Gavin's eyes flicked to the biker with a black eye and he saw that he was holding a sawed-off shotgun. Bendis stood up and opened the cooler and a cloud of flies took to wing. The meat inside was mangled almost beyond recognition but Gavin could still tell that it had once been human.

When Bendis flung a handful of it out over the surface of the water Gavin saw a ring, still attached to a severed finger, wink briefly in the boat's electric light. A moment later something enormous thundered out from the dark water and snapped its jaws shut and then fell back.

"They'll drag you down, if they get you," Bendis said. "I feed 'em every night but that don't mean they're tame. If they get a hold of you they'll never let you go."

One of them drifted into the boat's light. Reptilian eyes glowing green, jutting out just above the surface. Jaws cracked open in a smile that corresponded to no feeling that lived in the heart of man. Gavin moved away from the side of the boat, but Jesus, the whole thing was barely eight feet across. There wasn't anywhere on it that was out the reach of the gators. This was fucking nuts.

Bendis threw more chum onto the surface of the lake and the gators started churning up the water, fighting over it. Eventually the cooler was empty. The sound of those enormous bodies rolling over and over in the water was amazingly loud.

"Okay," Bendis said. His hands were stained to the elbows with blood.

"Yeah, okay," Gavin said.

"You think you're tough, big guy?" the biker with the black eye said.

"I know you guys want something. Just tell me what it is."

"Maybe we just want to kill you," the biker said.

"Yeah, well, better shoot me, because if you try and feed me to your buddies I'm taking one of you with me."

Bendis smiled.

"Just tell me what you want," Gavin said. "I know I fucked up. I didn't mean any disrespect, okay? I thought you were going to kill that boy and I used to go with his sister, all right? Tell me what I got to do to make it right."

"We weren't going to kill him," Bendis said. "Can't kill Mr. Marvin. Oh no. But we sure as shit can kill you, Gavin."

"Tell me what you want," Gavin said. He glanced from the Bendis to the biker and back. "Just tell me what you want."

"I want my money," Bendis said. "I can't have that dipshit walking around not having paid me. You feel me? Someone's got to pay me. Until someone pays me, it's like, I don't know. The fucking universe is out of balance. Do you feel me, Gavin? Do you feel me?"

Gavin stayed perfectly still.

"So come work for me," Bendis said.

"No," Gavin said immediately.

Bendis's face changed.

"I'll get you the money," Gavin said. "What's the vig?"

"You can't get the money," Bendis said.

"I'll get it."

"You can't, you lowlife," Gavin said. "Everyone you've ever met in your life ain't worth that much."

"I'll get it, Alan."

"Work it off."

"I can't do that, Alan."

"Sure you can."

"I can't. I won't. I'd rather die. I I won't do it."

Bendis raised his bloody hands forward, as if he was offering an embrace. Now he was smiling, and he looked awfully similar to the gators in the lake.

"Is that right?" he said softly.

Gavin heard the snick of the shotgun behind him.

A car horn honked. Bendis looked past Gavin to the shore and frowned. Gavin looked too and he saw something he didn't understand. A big car, a Hummer or a Jeep, was parked next to the bikers' clubhouse with its headlights shining across the lake. Someone was honking the car horn and someone else was standing silhouetted against the car's headlights, like Kristy had been earlier in the night. Only whoever that person was, he was really big. Enormous.

"You gotta be kidding me," Bendis said.

The horn honked and honked and honked. Then it stopped, and the enormous man moved out of the headlights. The Jeep or the Hummer reversed away from the lake and drove off.

"You have got to be kidding me," Bendis said. "Man."

He shook his head, frustrated, and then waved one bloody hand at the biker, who fired up the fan.

Gavin looked at Bendis. He knew he shouldn't do anything, anything at all, to question good fortune like this, but he couldn't keep the inquiry out of his eyes.

Bendis smirked and said nothing.

Two days later Gavin visited Todd. On Tuesday nights he coached wrestling and BJJ in Gainesville and the bus stopped near the Marvin residence. It was after ten when he ran the front doorbell.

Mr. Marvin opened the door and looked at him with surprise and displeasure.

"What are you doing here?" he asked.

No conceivable lie would fit.

"Kristy asked me to check up on Todd."

"She didn't think I can do that?"

Same thing again.

"No sir," Gavin said. "I don't think she does."

"Well, suit yourself son," Mr. Marvin said, and walked away from the open door back to the babbling television. "I'd be curious to know what in the hell you thought you were accomplishing. Only, I'm not."

Gavin pulled off his shoes without undoing his laces by stepping on the backs of his heels. He put down his gym bag and walked over to the door to the basement. Some kind of driving electronic music came faintly through the wood. There was no answer to his knock. Gavin rattled the knob but it was locked. Mr. Marvin was watching the television and didn't look up.

Gavin went outside and cut around the house until he came to one of the basement windows, half hidden by the long green grass. He knelt down and peered through. Inside, Todd was hunched over his small child's desk reading a book next to a laptop computer. Dirty dishes were scattered around; particularly mugs, for some reason. The bed was dishevelled and looked grimy and posters covered every square inch of the walls.

At first, he didn't see the cat curled up in a ball on the bed. He only noticed it when it opened its eyes. It stared him down, and then it opened its mouth in a meow that Gavin couldn't hear. Todd looked at the cat, then turned his head and looked at the window. He started when he saw Gavin and got to his feet and walked out of the bedroom.

Gavin looked back at the cat, but it had put its head down and was, to all appearances, asleep once more.

After a moment Gavin heard the door bang open and Todd stalked into view. He was wearing dirty black jeans and a faded t-shirt with small holes in the armpits that looked like they'd been gnawed by a mouse. A mixture of indignation and curiosity was on his face.

"What are you doing here?"

"You sister asked me to check in on you. I just got back from Gainesville."

Todd made a short, sharp noise that mainly conveyed contempt. Whether this contempt was direct at Gavin, Gainesville, or Kristy, it was impossible to say. Probably Todd himself didn't know.

"I don't need anyone checking up on me."

"Yes you do," Gavin said.

Todd looked at Gavin carefully in the eyes.

"Do you think you'll get back with my sister again if you're nice to me? Is that it?"

"You don't think I'd hang out with you just for your company?"

"She didn't go out with you because you were nice. I kind of think that was the whole appeal. That you weren't a nice guy. If she wants a nice guy, there are a lot of nice guys out there with a whole lot more to offer than you."

Gavin frowned a bit.

"You know, I don't expect thanks, I don't expect anything. But I saved your life."

"So what? You only did It for her. You don't give a damn about me."

"What difference does that ..."

"I remember what you were like to me. You were a thug. You used to call me sweetheart, all the time. When Kristy wasn't around to hear you. Sometimes when she was. 'Gavin, stop that,' she'd say." Here Todd made his voice sound high-pitched, female, but amused. "She wasn't looking out for me back then, was she? She was ashamed of me in high school."

"She was just a kid."

"So was I," Todd said, and there was a darkness in his voice, a deep pit, that for a moment made Gavin feel something like empathy. "Now she feels guilty. Maybe you do too? I don't think so somehow. Either way, I don't need your pity."

"Jesus Todd," Gavin said. "You go around with your balls in a twist because no one likes you. Well, you're not likeable. All right? Fuck."

Todd looked at him with this frozen, hurt, contemptuous look.

"Just come for a walk, or something, all right?" Gavin said.

"I'm busy."

"No you are fucking not. Your books will wait. Come on. Just get some fresh air, all right?"

Todd stood for a moment, looking mulish, and then he walked down the street and Gavin followed.

"He wasn't going to kill me," Todd said. "I think he was just going to scare me."

"He was scaring you, all right."

To this, Todd said nothing.

"What makes you so sure he wasn't going to kill you?"

"Never mind."

"You got someone looking out for you, huh?"

"No."

"Sure you do. He's looking out for me too. Your banker was going to feed me to the gators. Someone came up in a big car and he let me go."

Todd glanced at Gavin and then looked away. They were walking down the sidewalk in the lush green suburb, everything lit up by orange fluorescent light.

"Well," Gavin said, "you may have a buddy higher up on the food chain than Bendis. But you better watch yourself. Bendis doesn't like the idea of people thinking there's someone out there that borrowed from him and didn't pay him back. Even if somebody else did pay him back on your behalf."

"Where are you getting all this from?"

"It's not hard to figure out."

They stopped working.

"Anyway, be careful."

"All right," Todd said.

"What the fuck did you need two hundred large for?"

"Never mind."

"I mean, it must be drugs. Right?"

"Books," Todd said.

"Two hundred large for books?" Gavin said, stupefied.

"Ancient books," Todd said. "Magic tomes."

"Magic tomes?" Gavin cried. "For that kind of money you could have gone to Miami. Shit, you could have gone to Seattle. Anywhere where there are, you know. You wouldn't be alone."

"I'm always going to be alone," Todd said.

"You can make it that way if you want," Gavin said.

"It's the way it is." Todd looked down at some rainwater, pooled in the gutter behind a little mound of dirt. Then he reached down with his toe and dug a little canal so the water rushed free into the sewer.

"It was a little after you and Kristy broke up that Dad sent me to the camp," Todd said. His voice had a queer hollow quality, like it was a long distance call from far away. "Before he sent me, we had this talk. It was the nicest my Dad ever spoke to me. He said if I could just do this one thing, just this one thing for me, he wouldn't ask anything else. He wouldn't complain about the D&D or the music or the haircuts or anything. He was … he was desperate. It was the only time it showed that he loved me."

Gavin looked away. He felt embarrassed about something.

"I didn't know what to say," Todd said. "I just cried. Then he sent me away."

They walked a little further down the road.

"What'd they do to you?" Gavin asked.

Todd made a face.

"Did they hit you?"

"Sure. A lot of It was shocks."

"Shocks?"

"Like, electric."

"Jesus," Gavin said.

"Don't talk to be me about Jesus," Todd said. He stopped walking. "Go home, Gavin."

"I'm sorry Todd, but that's over now."

"No it's not."

"Sure it is. You and me, we're not so different, really. We had some rough times but we've got our whole lives ahead of us."

Todd actually smiled a little, he looked away, then looked back.

"Maybe you have changed," Todd said. "But it's not over for me, Gavin, and it won't ever be. It's not the hitting or the shocking or the … or the other things. It's how they make you feel about yourself.

Once they get in there, they get in you, things are never the same. Even when you get them out, you can't ever forget that they were in there."

"It's not going to be like it was before," Gavin said. "But that doesn't mean it's always got to be like it is now. It can get better."

Todd smiled now, but his smile had become unpleasant.

"You're right about that, buddy boy."

He turned and walked home and left Gavin standing alone in the artificial orange light.

The bell rang and the kids rushed the doors. It was amazing how fast they got out. For Gavin, it was the best part of the day. None of them seemed burdened or troubled. The wonderful thing about kids in high school was that they could still have a feeling that was pure; whether it was good or bad, at least it wasn't mixed up with anything else.

He watched them go, leaning up against the door to the supply room, and when things settled down (it only took a few moments) he pulled the bucket and the mop out of the closet and started to clean the floors.

Mrs. Monte, a black woman in her fifties with an impressively tottering tower of black and silver hair, was one of the last teachers to leave.

"You have a good weekend Mr. Rollins," she said.

"Yes ma'am," Gavin replied.

An hour and a half passed. Gavin was in the washroom attacking some graffiti scrawled on the side of toilet paper dispenser when the washroom door banged open.

Heavy but graceful footfalls. The clacking of men's dress shoes on the tiles. And then a polite but firm knock on the plastic stall door.

Gavin opened it and looked up.

"Mr. Rollins," the man said.

The man was about six and half feet tall and as wide and solid as a side of frozen beef hanging from a metal hook. An expression of patient professionalism. Scalp gleaming. Sunglasses indoors.

"Can I help you?" Gavin asked.

"My name is Henry. Mr. Greenberg wants to see you."

"Okay," Gavin said. "Let me just put ..."

"No," Henry said.

"Okay," Gavin said.

He followed the big, silent man outside to his enormous gleaming black Hummer. It was so high off the ground a little step folded out when Gavin opened the door. Inside the seats were made with leather, the windshields were tinted and possibly bulletproof. The stereo started blasting the Dixie Chicks when Henry turned the key.

They took the 100 east for forty five minutes. The Dixie Chicks kept playing; it was a CD. When it reached the end it started over again. Gavin looked out the window at the lush green trees, the sprawling ferns, the sudden crashings in the foliage that betrayed some creature moving in the wild.

Eventually they arrived at an enormous, sprawling mansion a stone's throw from the banks of the St. John's River, where the grass and the reeds were waving with the little breezes that moved along the surface of the water.

"Here we are," Henry said amiably, and turned the car off. Gavin missed the step on the way out and stumbled on the flawless black asphalt.

It was the biggest house he'd ever seen. Painted white, enormous pillars on the front porch, twelve foot windows. Like something from another era.

They took a path made of ground seashells through a large garden. A pair of Hispanic gardeners walked past them, one of them pushing a wheelbarrow that contained a little tree. The path wound down among the flowers and fountains and the little grey stone sculptures to a wooden bench that rested at the top of a hill, before the earth plunged away towards the water.

Despite the sweltering evening heat, and the sun pressing down from behind them, the old man sitting on the bench was wrapped in a warm blanket. Henry stopped walking but gestured for Gavin to go on. He did so, cautiously, circling around the side.

When Greenberg saw him, he motioned Gavin over weakly with one claw-like hand.

"I'm not going to bite you, Rollins."

Greenberg was incredibly, incredibly old. His skin was as dry and brittle as paper, his hair was as white and fine as spider webs. His face was so wrinkled and collapsed in on itself that he looked more like a monkey than a human being. An oxygen tank lay between his skinny knees and every few breaths Greenberg would raise the mask to his face to take a deep breath. A little yarmulke was perched at an almost jaunty angle on the top of his head.

Gavin carefully sat down on the bench. There was plenty of room; Greenberg was as skinny as a rake.

"Ooh-gah, ooh-gah," Greenberg wheezed into his mask. When he turned to look at Gavin, his eyes were sharp and clear.

"You're a Canadian I hear? Came down on a scholarship?"

"That's right."

"Prize fighter, huh?"

"Not anymore."

"Boxing was a great racket," Greenberg said, "back in my day. Now they've ruined it. Too many belts." Greenberg shook his head. "And this cage fighting thing the kids are into. Men rolling around on each other in their shorts. Wrapping their legs around each other. It's all owned by the casinos."

Greenberg started to cough and put his mask over his mouth.

"Of course," Greenberg said, his voice slightly muffled by the mask, "we used to run the casinos too! This was all a long time ago, probably before you were born."

Gavin nodded.

"Why didn't you go back to Canada if you're not a prize fighter anymore?"

"There's nothing for me up there."

"And there is here?"

To this, Gavin said nothing.

"Go up the ledge there and look down," Greenberg said through his mask.

Gavin did so. He saw a fenced pen, perhaps twenty-five feet square. Sunning itself in the mud, contentedly staring at nothing with an effortless air of malice, was the biggest alligator he'd ever seen.

He backed away and looked at Greenberg, who had taken the mask away from his mouth and was watching Gavin with a little twinkle in his sunken, rheumy, intelligent eyes.

"I brought that crocodile here with me in 1962," Greenberg rasped. "That's forty-eight years ago. I'm not sure how old he was when I got him. They say the oldest crocodile in the world is one hundred and thirty years old. I wonder how long it's going to last." Greenberg was silent for a moment and then he finally said: "It's funny to think it's going to last longer than me. It was just a joke. Benny gave it to me. They used to call me the crocodile, for a while. I didn't like it so I told them to stop. And they did, except for Benny. Funny how he wouldn't listen to me, considering how he got when people called him by his nickname. Of course, look what happened to him in the end."

Greenberg put the mask back over his mouth and breathed. He seemed to shrink into himself, and stared off into nothing.

Gavin sat back down on the bench.

"They all thought they were pretty hard cases. Oh yes. Only, where are they now?" Greenberg looked at Gavin steadily with one reptilian eye. "All gone. Most of them didn't make it ten years past RICO. Some of them thought I was too soft, too ... phlegmatic. Do you know what that means?"

"No," Gavin said.

Greenberg shrugged and looked away. "The smart ones knew different. That's why they called me the crocodile. They can go for weeks without even moving. They slow their heart down and just lie in the mud. Till their moment comes."

Gavin rested his elbows on his knees and dangled his hands between his legs.

Ooh-gah. Ooh-gah.

Their shadows stretched out in front of them. Gavin thought of the crocodile down there in its little pen, waiting with ancient and inhuman patience since 1962.

"Now, this," Greenberg said, motioning to the oxygen tank. "There's no defence against it at all. Nothing I can do."

"We all have to die sometime," Gavin said.

"Do we?" Greenberg replied.

"I don't know."

Greenberg coughed and put the mask back over his face.

"In all my years I never saw anything to make me believe there's something after this life," he said through the mask. "But I can't go without a fight. If there's anything out there, no matter how stupid it seems, I have to look into it. It's not my nature to just accept something like this."

Greenberg put the mask down.

"Anyway, what else am I going to do with my time."

"Are you saying you're trying to find a way to live forever?"

"Not forever, necessarily," Greenberg said. "Just a little while longer."

"Holy shit," Gavin said. "Did you give Todd Marvin 200 large to look in magic tomes for the fountain of youth for you?"

Greenberg smiled a little. "You think it's a waste?"

"I guess you can't take it with you."

"Precisely."

"Why didn't you just give it to him directly? Why go through Bendis?"

"I have a reputation to maintain. I am still only semi-retired. I can't give people the idea I'm cracking up."

Ooh-gah. The old man's eyes grew soft and unfocussed when he inhaled the oxygen.

"Well, why don't you get that psychopath Bendis to take it easy on Todd?"

"Mr. Bendis is a blunt instrument," Greenberg said. "Overly concerned with his reputation. But, after all, if the ruse that the money came from him is to be maintained, he can hardly remain indifferent in the face of Mr. Marvin's failure to pay him back."

"Oh Christ," Gavin said, and put his right hand over his mouth.

"There's no arrangement between Mr. Marvin and myself, of course. I heard he was seeking to acquire certain texts and that he had begun approaching some unsavoury figures for financing. I just ensured that one of them would lend to him. But Mr. Marvin has failed to produce any results."

"Results?" Gavin said. "The fountain of youth?"

"Results of any kind."

"Mr. Greenberg, with all due respect, this is nuts."

The corner of the old man's mouth moved, just a little.

"And yet," he said, "here we are."

"Fine," Gavin said. "What do you want from me?"

"I know your type," Greenberg said in his leathery voice, and fixed Gavin once more with that sidewise predatory glance. "Ex-boxer. Seen plenty of them in my day. You're a desperate breed. You'll hang around no matter the beating you take, just looking for that one miracle punch to bring you back into it."

Ooh-gah.

"I don't want anything from you, Rollins," Greenberg continued. "I just want you to know that if your girl's brother doesn't come through for me, he's probably going to die. And now my eye has fallen upon you. Govern yourself accordingly."

"Okay, but what do you want? What do you want me to do?"

Ooh-gah. Greenberg looked back at the river.

"We threw a man into that crocodile pen, once," Greenberg said. "The croc just stared at him while he screamed and screamed for help. We shot him, to shut him up, and then the croc waddled over and ate him after he was dead." Greenberg shook his head. "Hell of a thing."

Gavin stood up and walked back towards the setting sun with his hands dug down into his pockets. The enormous bodyguard was waiting for him and they trudged back up the hill to the Hummer in silence.

Gavin came into the Starbucks hungry after practice but when he saw there were no doughnuts, only absurdly expensive little buns, he just ordered a coffee. She was late, of course, and since Gavin had arrived ten minutes early he was kept waiting a long time.

"I'm sorry Gavin," she said as she dropped her purse off. "I'll be back, I'm just going to get something."

He waited while she stood in line. Her order seemed unbelievably complicated. She came back with something that had whipped cream on the top.

"So good to see you again," she said. She smiled, with real but faint warmth, like coals from a big fire the night before.

"Nice to see you too," Gavin said.

"Dad was telling me you've been to see Todd a couple of tImes."

"Yeah."

"I guess he's doing a little better these days, but we've seen calm times before."

"The only way you can tell if someone's really changed is time," Gavin said, trying to keep his voice steady.

"That's very true," Kristy said. She was looking all around the coffee shop. It wasn't that she was uncomfortable; she wasn't. It wasn't that she didn't want to look at him either. It was just that a lot of the stuff in here was more interesting to her than him.

"Well, look, the reason I called you ..."

"Before you say anything," Kristy said, "I just wanted to say thanks, but you don't have to keep visiting him."

"What?"

"I really appreciate it," Kristy said. "But I was talking with Trevor and it's too much for me to ask. I just feel so guilty because I'm not there. But Todd's a grown man now, and there's nothing we can do for him. Even if we watched him twenty-four hours a day. He just has to figure it out for himself. You've already done so much for him. You even risked your life. I don't want you to feel like you have to stay there and look out for him. Just for me."

She drank her coffee and Gavin looked away. He felt as if his tether had been cut and he was just floating away.

"Well," he started. For a moment he couldn't think of anything more to say. "Well the thing is, Kristy, is that he owes a lot of money. More than he can pay back."

Kristy shook her head. "I don't even want to know. If he's in trouble he should go to the police. I probably should have just called the police last time, instead of risking your life like that. I'm sorry for that Gavin. I was so focused on what he needed I forgot to think of the risk to you. Or even to me. I can't live my life for other people. And neither should you."

"Okay."

"What did you call me here to talk about?"

"Just about your brother," Gavin said.

"Is there anything I can really do though? Really?"

She looked at him earnestly and he felt a sinking feeling in his stomach. He took a deep breath.

"I guess not."

"I just don't want you to feel like I did," Kristy said. "Like you're living for someone else."

She put her hand on his.

"But thank you Gavin. You really have changed. I'm proud of you."

Gavin thought of himself a few years ago, juiced on steroids, cut like a marble statute, in the clubs every night, looking for women, looking for fights.

"Thanks Kristy. I know I wasn't always good to you."

"No," she said, and smiled that crooked smile he remembered. "You sure weren't."

He was trudging to a meeting without one grain of hope in his soul when his cell phone rang. Call display showed the Marvin Residence.

"Hello?"

"Gavin, it's me."

"Mr. Marvin."

"Gavin, I ... I need your help."

The old man sounded lost. Proud and humble at the same time. As if expecting a rebuff. As well he might.

"You need my help?"

"I ... I had a fight with Todd. He ran off."

Gavin waited and said nothing, partially because he could not trust himself to speak, partly because he had no idea what to say.

"He just ... he just sits there reading those un-Christian books with all that weird writing, in Latin, or something, and his friends with the long hair and the earrings and the goddamned leather collars and ... I just lost my temper. Only this time it was different, and he knocked me down. I'm not as young as I used to be. And he stomped around the place and smashed everything and he left and he said he wasn't coming back."

Gavin was standing on the shoulder of the highway holding the phone to his ear. It would have felt good just to flip the phone shut and keep walking, but he felt like he was paying for something by listening. A debt owed to somebody, other than the charming Marvin family, a debt that he felt like he was going to be paying back for a long time to come.

There was a moment of silence, and then Marvin spoke again:

"Gavin? Are you there?"

"Yeah. I'm here."

"The thing is, he has a meeting with his parole officer. Tomorrow morning. At 9 o'clock, sharp. If he doesn't make it ..."

"Mr. Marvin," Gavin said when, all of a sudden, he couldn't take it anymore. "What would you do, right now, if you were me?"

The silence spun out for a few more moments.

"Son, I just don't have anyone else to call. No one else in the world. That's all."

For a little while, Gavin thought he wouldn't be able to take it. He got angrier and angrier and more and more frustrated and he thought he might yell or throw his phone away or just leave – leave everything, leave the whole world. It was this last thought that calmed him down. There was nowhere to go. After a moment he wasn't even angry anymore. He just felt empty and used and hopeless.

"What the hell do you want me to do?"

"Just talk to him. Just get him to his parole meeting tomorrow, even if he doesn't come back home."

"Why will he listen to me?"

"I don't know."

"Where is he?"

"I don't know. He ran off."

"Well, what the fuck, Mr. Marvin?"

"Him and his fag friends are always hanging around this abandoned house on 84. About a mile south of Highway 193. There's a path through the forest to an old house at the top of the hill."

Gavin did not say anything. He could feel his cell phone warping under his grip. Where was all this anger coming from? It was supposed to be gone.

"You can borrow my car," Mr. Marvin said.

Highway 84 was a small road that didn't really go anywhere except to some more ponds and swamps and trees. No lights were by the side of the road and all was clothed in darkness. The car's headlights pointed down into the road and only illuminated a few feet ahead.

The house was difficult to see against the dark night sky. He caught sight of it when the clouds moved off the moon and everything was lit up silver. The ditches were full of reeds and tall grass, and the hill was forested and carpeted with ferns. At the top of the hill, the house itself was ruined and run down, sagging in on itself, roped with vines and moss.

Gavin stopped the car, got out, and walked to the path. The water rushed over the top of his shoes and the reeds rustled around him as he pushed his way through the ditch and started up the hill, with the ferns brushing against his shins and knees. He reached up and laid his hands on the trees to steady himself on the treacherous ground. At the top of the hill the house loomed over him, grim and ancient and wounded. It was very quiet, away from the road.

Inside it was almost pitch black. A staircase headed up to the second floor. On his left and right were empty rooms, with trash and empty beer bottles scattered on the floor. Graffiti was scribbled on the walls, fuck this, faggot that, nigger you. Somebody loves someone else.

Gavin walked down the hallway to the back of the house. The shattered window looked out into a fern-covered field. A scurrying noise coming from the chimney. A kitchen with rusted sinks and brown, evil-looking stains spreading across the wall. And a door with a latch bolted onto it (new) and an open padlock hanging from it (also new).

He opened the door. Rickety wood steps descended down into darkness that was not quite complete. Gavin was not an imaginative or superstitious man and he was not afraid. He tromped downstairs.

Two men were in the basement. One was Todd.

"Who's that?" Todd cried, his voice afraid.

"It's Gavin."

"Who's that?"

"Jesus Christ, it's me, Gavin Rollins. Okay?"

"Gavin?"

Todd wore something like a black bathrobe. His face was slick with sweat and his hair was standing up like he'd been running his hands through it. The basement was lit with dozens of big, thick candles, whose slender flames danced skittishly with every little breath of air.

The walls of the basement were damp concrete and they were covered with writing in chalk. Foreign languages and arcane symbols that worked together to form subtle patterns that shimmered through all of the superficial chaos, squirming into some kind of frightening order before dissolving back into random scribbling. A shelf of books rested in the back corner, and a tray next to Todd bore various instruments: knives, wands, crucifixes, vials of murky liquid.

A forty pound bag of rock salt sat on the ground next to the tray. It was open. A circle of salt had been poured on the floor. Standing in this circle was the second man.

"Jesus Gavin," Todd said. "You scared the fuck out of me."

"C'mon Todd," Gavin said gently. "Let's get out of here."

"How did you find me?"

"It's late. You need to get up tomorrow morning."

The second man was looking at Gavin. Not staring, exactly. It was more of a steady gaze. His eyes were wide and green and sensitive. He had long brown hair tied in a pony-tail behind his head and a wispy beard. His face was lean, almost narrow, with a prominent nose and a small, pursed mouth. He was wearing a plain grey t-shirt, a pair of sweatpants, and sandals.

"I can't come now," Todd said. "Are you crazy? Look ..." Todd gestured at the second man and then stopped. He laughed shakily. "You changed again."

"Todd," Gavin said, the gentleness draining out of his voice. "Stop fucking around. You can play with your buddy here tomorrow night."

"It's not my buddy," Todd said. "He's a demon."

"No, he isn't," Gavin said. "Look, I'm trying to be understanding, I am, with your fucking ... bullshit here. But it's not in my nature, Todd. It just isn't. So pack up your shit, and let's go, before I lose my temper."

"I can't," Todd said. "Do you know who this is?"

"It's one of your fag friends, Todd. I can see who it is."

"Don't talk to me like that!" Todd shrieked. "I did it! Can't you say! They said I couldn't do it, but I did! And now all of you are going to pay!"

"Okay Todd," Gavin said. "How about this? I'm going to drag you out of here. If you know magic, use it to stop me. I'll give you one minute."

Todd's face fell.

"I need to stay here."

"Fine, Todd. Use your magic. If all this is real, use your magic."

"I ... it's very dangerous."

"I'm a tough guy. I can take it."

"The thing is," Todd said. "I summoned the demon, but, I ... I can't make it do anything. I think ... I think it might be the wrong one. I opened this, this door, you see, and it came through when I invoked this name. That's how you control them. You can make them do what you say if you know their name."

"Thirty seconds Todd."

"I need more time!" Todd screamed. "Fuck you! Can't you see what that is?"

"I see a lot of shit I don't give a fuck about, Todd," Gavin said, and stepped forward.

"Wait, wait!" Todd said. "Okay, I'll come with you. Okay? Fuck you! I'll come. Just let me send it back."

"I'm so tired of this."

"Just one spell! It'll take five minutes."

The man in the circle didn't say anything. His glance flipped between Todd and Gavin.

"You have five minutes to finish your game," Gavin said.

Todd swallowed. He opened a book and set it on his tray. After a moment he started to read and gesture with his hands. His voice grew louder, and although Gavin could not understand the language, it seemed as if Todd was repeating himself. His hands wove a hypnotic rhythm in the air. He lifted some silver instruments and closed his eyes and titled his head back and let out a tremendous shout.

The man in the circle of salt watched patiently.

When Todd finished he was gasping for air. He tilted his head back down and opened his eyes and looked at the man and said: "He's still here!"

"He sure is, Todd," Gavin said.

"Why is he still here?"

"Let's go, Todd."

"But Gavin, we can't! Don't you see!"

"We had a deal," Gavin said, with a flat, final tone of voice.

"That's a demon!" Todd screamed. "Don't you get it? I called him here, and I can't make it do anything, it just sits there, and looks at me! Don't you fucking get it, you idiot? We can't go anywhere until I figure this out."

The rage that had been building in Gavin suddenly found an outlet. He stormed in towards Todd and caught him by the front of his robe and jerked his jaw in towards his fist.

"Help!" Todd screamed, and the pathetic sound of his voice, of course, only further enraged Gavin. He threw Todd down on the ground and sat on his chest and winged in punches.

"It's not a fucking demon, you faggot!" Gavin shouted.

"Help! Help!" Todd screamed. "Stop it, stop it!"

"I saved your life, you idiot!" Gavin screamed. "Half the fucking gangsters in Florida are after me because of you! I saved your life! Your fucking life! All I ask is that you don't waste it, that you don't be such a fucking loser!"

A punch sailed in and crunched Todd's nose flat against his face. Previously he'd only been raising red, twisted wells. Now there was an explosion of blood. Todd's voice rose up to a high shriek and he started to gasp and cry, screaming and wailing and choking sobs and great almost shouted "ah ha ha ha" noises.

"Stop it! Stop it!"

Gavin held his fists in front of his eyes and he felt a deep, deep loathing for himself. So deep inside, so far buried beneath anything he had ever had the courage to show himself, let alone anyone else, that he had never known until now how it had underpinned all his life and all his works. He listened to Todd cry and watched him choke on his own blood that was flowing back into his throat and go into hysterics. Then he reached down and pressed down on either side of Todd's windpipe.

Todd thrashed around desperately for a moment and then fell unconscious. Gavin released him and stood up and lifted him onto his shoulders.

He glanced at the silent man in the circle.

"Hey," the man suddenly said. "Can I come with you?"

"Fine," Gavin said. "Pack up your shit."

Gavin struggled a little under Todd's weight as he walked to the stairs.

"Wait," the man said.

"Nope," Gavin said. "You can come now or walk."

"Wait," the man said again in a very calm, reasonable voice.

Gavin turned around to get his foot on the stairs. In doing so, he looked back at the man and could see that he had walked right up to the edge of the circle.

"Just break this circle," the man said.

"You too? Hey, fuck you asshole," Gavin snarled. He was tired and sickened with the whole situation. Blood was running out of Todd's smashed nose down the back of his pant legs. "You want to come, get your ass over here."

"I can't go till you break the circle," the man said. "Just break it."

Gavin started climbing the stairs.

"Don't leave me here man, just break the circle. It's not much to ask."

And then right when Gavin reached the top:

"Think about if there's anything you want."

Gavin made his way back to the front door and out of the house. Halfway down the hill, Todd woke up and stirred.

"Whad's going on?" he said, voice muffled by his injury.

Gavin didn't reply. He glanced once over his shoulder at the house. No one was following him.

"Weirdos," he said to himself.

Two days later Gavin was at home in his trailer, drinking Pepsi and watching TV, when his cell phone rang. His call display read: "County of Alachua's Sherriff's Office."

"Hello?" he said.

There was a lot of background noise, men talking and shouting, and then a voice he did not recognize said:

"Gavin?"

"Yeah."

"It's Todd."

"Todd? Where are you calling from?"

"Jail."

"Jail? Why are you in jail? Didn't you go to your ..."

"Yes, I went," Todd said. "And I failed my drug test."

"You what?"

"I tested positive for pot."

"Oh, what the fuck."

"I wasn't even supposed to be at that hearing," Todd said in his clogged-up voice while things banged and crashed away in the background. "I was supposed to be free. Free of all you people. Because of you I'm in here!"

"Why were you smoking pot when you knew you had a parole hearing, you idiot?" Gavin said.

Todd made quiet little noises that Gavin could barely hear over the background noise.

"Todd? Stay strong now. You've got to be strong."

"I'm not strong though," Todd said. "I'm not strong enough."

"Yes you are. God doesn't put you through anything he doesn't give you the strength to bear. You can do it. Okay? Keep your chin up."

"Gavin, what happened with the demon?"

"I left your buddy in the basement."

"Did you lock the door?"

"No, I didn't lock the door."

"You have go back!" Todd said. "You have to make sure that door is locked. Don't talk to it when you go back. Don't listen to anything it says. Just go back and lock the door right away."

"Todd, forget it."

"Listen to me!"

"No, you listen to me Todd, all right? There are no demons or angels or anything like that. Everything is what it is. You're stuck with this life. Okay? It's the only life there is. You have to start making the most of it."

"I hate this life," Todd said. "I hate it and I hate you! I wish you'd let me die."

"Fuck you, asshole. Fuck everything about you."

Gavin hung up. He looked back at the television screen.

Another two days passed, and again Gavin was alone at home in his trailer, watching the television. It was early in the morning and he had the day off. His hands were neatly folded across his chest and he was wearing nothing but his underwear. Neither Kristy nor Mr. Marvin had called him since the night he had brought Todd home. The seconds were tick, tick, ticking past.

In his mind he saw a thin stream of Jagermeister pouring into a frosted shot glass. Brown bottles of beer. A martini shaker, rattling ice cubes.

He tried to turn his mind to other things, but what else was there?

One thing, he supposed – those soft eyes, that voice, those words:

Think about if there's anything you want.

It kept coming back to his mind. That loser in his track pants, standing in the circle of salt, just looking at him.

"Well, so what?" he said.

And he looked back at the TV.

And he remembered how he'd felt in the basement. Looking at his fists. Todd screaming and screaming. *Anything you want.*

What he had told Todd was the truth. There was no world other than this one. There was no escape, other than death. So it was more boredom than anything else that compelled him outside in his sneakers and windbreaker and onto the highway, walking on the shoulder to the northwest, back to the old ruined house.

It was a warm, sunny day and by the time he reached his destination his shirt was stuck to his back with sweat. The house was still there, of course, crouched at the top of the hill like a sentry of a forgotten race, as sinister as ever in the sunshine. Gavin spent a little time looking at it. A strange feeling was coiling around in his chest. He didn't know why he was here, or what he expected to find.

It would be a relief to see that the basement was empty.

A porcupine slithered underneath the porch as he went through the front door. The house seemed to smell worse. It certainly looked dirtier than he remembered it. The light that streamed through the windows was faded and distant.

The stairs creaked under his feet as he walked down into the basement. It was almost pitch black, he should have brought a flashlight, but some faint light came through the cracked and stained windows near the ceilings.

And the man was there, standing in the circle of salt, wearing the same clothes.

"Hey man," the stranger said.

Gavin said nothing for a moment.

The stranger came right up to the edge of the circle of salt.

"How are you doing?"

Gavin opened his mouth, and closed it again.

"Did you think of anything you want? Anything at all?"

"I don't believe you," Gavin said. "I don't believe this."

"Okay," the stranger said. "Could you break this circle? Could you do that for me?"

Gavin didn't move.

"I don't see what it could hurt, if you don't believe in magic."

"It couldn't hurt anything at all," Gavin said. "I just don't see what I get out of it."

"Tell me what you want."

"You can't give me anything," Gavin said.

"Well, if that's true, than there's no harm in breaking the circle."

Now the stranger smiled, only a little. His expression of calm intensity never wavered.

Gavin took a few steps forward. He saw that a pentagram was drawn in chalk on the floor in the circle. And he saw red splatters that could be rust or dirt or blood.

"It's a nice, even circle," the stranger said. "Good thick line. Not a little crack. Just run your finger through it for me, Gavin. Can you do that?"

The man was perfectly ordinary. Everything was ordinary about him except that he was here.

"So you're saying you're a demon."

"Demon, well. That's a word. I'm something though, aren't I? You see me?"

"I think so."

"Okay," the man said. "So we know I'm something. But you don't know what. I look just like a person though, right?"

Nothing was down here that had not been here before. No food wrappers, no water bottles, no clothes, no puddles of urine or little piles of feces. The man's clothes did not appear to be sweaty or dirty.

"But if I was a person, I could just walk out of here on my own. Right? Which I can't seem to do."

"I don't know you can't."

"But if I'm not a person, Gavin, then I might be in a position to help you with something."

"With what?"

"Well, what do you want?"

Gavin looked at the man for a long time.

"I'm not telling you what I want."

The man smiled, wider this time.

"That's very wise," he said. "If you tell someone what you want, you're really telling them who you are. You're telling them the greatest secret of all."

"Why don't you ... why don't you just step over that salt."

"I can't."

"Then, why don't you just go back to where you came from."

"I can't do that either." A larger smile, very large. Unfeigned confidence. No fear in him at all. Unsettling. "You see the bind I'm in."

Gavin licked his lips and took a step back.

"I wouldn't leave without helping me out if I were you."

"You think I'm scared of you?"

"Let me ask you something," the man said. "Do you think I will stay here forever, bound by only an inch of salt? Someone will let me out. Don't you want to be the one? Instead of the one that paraded around in front of me, and then left? Right now you have all the leverage. When this line breaks, you won't have any at all."

Gavin looked at the man for a while, and then he turned his head and spat.

"All right then," the man said. "Let's see how this works out for you. Remember though: it's not just by telling someone what you want that you tell them who you are. Everything you do does that. The way you stand, the way you talk. The way you looked at your fists after you broke that poor dope's nose. I know you, Gavin Rollins. I know your face, I know what's in your heart. I know your name. You're in my world now, on my radar. You just remember that."

The man paced back and forth a little in the circle of salt.

"You know that to understand one thing fully and completely you have to understand everything else? Right? To know what cat is, you have to know about the mice it eats, the grain the mice eat, the sun and the rain that allow the grain to grow. Everything. And conversely, to know one thing completely is to understand everything else. A cat. A flower. A fleeting expression on a baby's face. Tea leaves, the flight of bird, the random patters of an inkblot. Everything is in everything else. And so if you leave yourself open for one moment, that's maybe all someone needs. If they were looking carefully enough, I mean."

"You think you know me?

The man smiled a little.

"Sure I know you, Gavin. You aren't complicated. You think it's too late and it's all over and so you're just waiting. It isn't, you know. It's only thinking that makes it so. But then, it's no easier to change your thinking than anything else. And you can't do it, Gavin. You and I, we're both trapped. The difference is, one day, I'm going to get loose."

"I do not believe in you," Gavin said.

The man shrugged. He was starting to look a little bored.

"Well, I've got my eye on you, anyway. You know, normally, most of you look the same to us. Because you're so small. Not you though. Not you, anymore."

Gavin walked to the top of the stairs. As he was closing the door he thought: can I really lock that guy in the basement? He was just a man, after all. That's all he was.

"You come up here now," Gavin said, "or I'll lock the door."

"Don't lock it!" the man shouted from the darkness. "Leave it open."

"Then come up now."

"Don't lock it!" the man called.

"You come up now."

"Don't you lock me down here, Gavin! I'd be trapped! I'd starve!"

"I'm closing the door."

"Gavin! Gavin!"

Then as the lock was clicking shut:

"I could get her for you, Gavin. Just say the word."

That night he couldn't sleep. He felt as if he'd been sleeping his whole life and he'd only just woken up. That feeling, of something curling around inside him, got stronger and stronger.

He got a call Friday afternoon from the Marvin household when he was still at the school, cleaning the hardened chocolate milk and creamed corn off of the floor.

"What?"

"Gavin, it's me." Mr. Marvin. "I just wanted to say thank you for what you did. I don't know if I ever got a proper chance."

"Well, it wasn't anything. I'm sorry I lost my temper and I'm sorry it didn't end up working out."

"Well, that's just the thing. It ended up working out okay. We had a sentencing hearing just today."

"Already?"

"Todd pleaded guilty. And the judge, he wasn't one of these liberal activist judges. He was elected as a Christian. And I had a chance to stand up and talk about all of the troubles me and Todd had, on account of, well. You know. And I told him about some of the stuff that happened at Redeemer Christian Counselling. And the judge was pretty shocked. He said it gave Christians a bad name. Which it does, of course. I still think it was sending him there that pushed him over the edge. I truly think Todd could have gone either way but what they did to him was too harsh. It backfired. If you're too harsh, things can backfire. That's what I've come to realize."

"Did the judge let him off?"

"No, but he said he'd send him for more counselling. Todd could do that or jail. He recommended a different Christian counselling place, where they focus on the unconditional love of Jesus Christ. That's what he said. Unconditional love and forgiveness. And they do all sorts of counselling, drugs too. This is in Gainesville. So Todd's going there. I think it's for the best. I think that's what Todd needs. He just needs help because he's sick."

Gavin looked up at the ceiling. Right now, he was the one that felt sick, only he wasn't exactly sure why.

"Well," Gavin said. "That's good. He could have gone to jail for a long time."

"Yeah," Mr. Marvin said. "Maybe things are finally going to start turning around for us now."

"That'd be nice," Gavin said.

"Well," Mr. Marvin said. "Thanks anyway, is what I called to say."

"Where is Todd?"

"He's here. We're going to Gainesville tomorrow."

Gavin was quiet a moment, then he said:

"Can I talk to him?"

It took Mr. Marvin a moment to reply.

"Well, I'm not sure what kind of mood he's in."

"Just ask him for me."

"All right."

The phone went dead for a while. The only sound was the rattle of the cafeteria's air conditioner. It occurred to Gavin, suddenly and uncharacteristically, that he was all alone in the building and there was no one to hear him if he started to scream.

Clunking noises as someone picked up the phone on the other end.

"Hey," Todd said, subdued.

"Todd, I'm sorry they're sending you back."

"It's okay," Todd said. "This place doesn't sound as bad. I don't know. Maybe it'll work."

"Todd," Gavin said. "If there's a God, he made you the way you are for a reason. You don't need to be fixed. You're all right. I'm sorry for what we've all done to you."

"Whatever," Todd said. "It's not your fault."

A moment of silence, a thing unspoken.

"Todd, I went back three days later and your friend was still there."

"Yep," was all Todd said.

"I locked him down there."

"Good."

"Todd ..."

"I can't send it back," Todd said. "I don't know how. All that ... all that work. The money, the dreadful risk. And all it did was look at me. Stare. I tried for hours before you got there. I summoned the wrong thing, Gavin. I didn't know its name. I can't even send it back."

It was very quiet.

"Your friend ... I locked him in the basement," Gavin said.

"Well, good for you," Todd said.

The connection cut off.

That night he was awoken by the sound of breaking glass. First his window, then the Molotov cocktail shattering against the linoleum tiles of the kitchen of his trailer. A great whoosh of air, a blast of heat. Acrid, chemical smoke.

He stumbled out the door, as he was supposed to. They waited in a crescent while his trailer burned behind him and laughed at him as he stood half naked and half asleep in the moonlight and the humid night air.

Bendis was grinning. His hair hung down around his face because he was slouching a little bit as he dragged the sledgehammer along the ground behind him.

"I had to meet you here todaaaaaaaaaaaaaaaaaaaaaay," Bendis sang, "there's just so many things to saaaaaaaaaaaay."

"We can talk about this," Gavin said.

"Please don't stop me, till I'm throoooooooooooough...."

Something exploded from the trailer; a tank of gas, perhaps. The force of it hitting his back, the wave of searing heat.

"... this is something, I hate to dooooooooooo."

Gavin tried to run but two of the bikers closed the gap he'd been aiming for and wrestled him to the ground.

"We've been meeting here so loooooooooooong, I guess what we done, oh, was wroooooooooooong!"

The sound of the sledgehammer dragging along the ground stopped abruptly as it lifted up into the air.

"Bendis, for God's sake!"

Gavin tried to twist his head around to see what was happening but someone was sitting on his back. A moment later his right knee exploded in pain and he screamed at the top of his lungs, but the sound of his voice was lost in the roaring fire.

"Please darlin', don't you cryyyyyyyyyyyyyyy," Bendis bellowed. "Let's just kiss and say goodbyyyyyyyyyyyye!"

"No, no don't! Don't!" Gavin said, weeping in pain. "Fuck, no, don't Bendis! Don't!"

His other knee.

Gavin screamed and screamed into the ground. Then he scrunched up his face and closed his eyes and just stayed still.

The sledgehammer clattered down on the concrete a few feet away. Gavin's shoulder was seized roughly and they flipped him onto his back. He gasped in pain and opened his eyes and counted at least three shotguns pointed at his face.

Bendis knelt down next to him and grabbed him by one of his jug ears.

"You've got one week," Bendis said.

In spite of himself, Gavin let out a yelp of laughter.

"Are you retarded?" Gavin gasped.

"One week."

"Fucking shoot me, you piece of shit."

Bendis smiled and stood up.

"Fucking shoot me, I'm just going to tell the fucking cops who did this."

"Go ahead," Bendis said, and smiled. Truly insane. "Go ahead. It'll just be the Alabama chapter that finishes the job. Get me my money. One week."

The bikers left and Gavin closed his eyes. His breathing hitched in his chest.

In the ambulance Gavin could faintly hear the radio from the cab. It was playing "My Sweet Lord" by George Harrison.

Gavin thought that was pretty nice.

A week later Gavin was sitting in the living room of the Marvin household, playing with Todd's PSP. He was as high as a kite on painkillers and he couldn't get his fingers to work the buttons properly. His little character kept running in circles and falling down. Gavin laughed.

The drugs were amazing. He wasn't sure he'd felt this good in a long time. Not since he'd been sober, certainly, and a long time before.

It was the cat who noticed the visitor first. Gavin was alerted by the hissing. When he turned his head and looked up at the window, he saw Henry squatting by the basement window looking at him. His heart almost stopped in his chest.

"Jesus," he said.

Henry lifted his hand and made a little waving gesture.

"Okay," Gavin said.

He rolled the wheelchair over to the front door and unlocked. A moment later it opened inwards, gently, so Gavin had time to roll back from its path.

Henry came in with Mr. Greenberg cradled in his arms. Greenberg was thinner and he had spots on his wrists and his neck. His eyes rolled towards Gavin. They were yellow in the corners. Henry set him down in a chair and left.

"I'm sorry about your legs," Greenberg whispered. "That Bendis is an animal."

A smile. Then Greenberg said no more and struggled with his breath until his bodyguard returned with the oxygen tank.

Ooh-gah, ooh-gah.

Then Greenberg continued:

"The doctors said I shouldn't leave the hospital," he said, and smiled. "But then, what does it matter now, really? They're giving me days. I could die, sitting here. Me. I could die."

"Shit," Gavin said.

Greenberg's lips twisted in a smile.

"Nothing else has panned out."

"What were you expecting?"

"Except for you," Greenberg said. "You're my last hope. Do you have anything for me? Anything at all?"

"Nope," Gavin said.

Greenberg put his face back into the mask for a moment and then took it out again. His lips pulled back from his teeth: "I'll tell you what I told the others: save my life or pay your debts."

"What were you expecting?" Gavin said. "There's no such thing as magic."

"Too bad for you," Greenberg said, pointing at him, and then he began to cough and put the mask back to his face.

Henry stood at the back of the room and barely moved.

"I can tell you this because it doesn't matter anymore. You're dead. Bendis won't let up. He won't go away. You go to the cops and it won't make a difference. He'll take it out of you, every penny. So you're not going to outlive me by much. So it's too bad for you, there's no such thing as magic. Too bad ..." His voice dissolved into wretched coughing and he turned back to the mask.

When he was done inhaling oxygen, he dragged up an enormous gob of bloody phlegm and hacked it out onto the floor. Then he fixed Gavin with his crocodile gaze and said: "Last chance. For you, and for me."

Gavin looked back, with his head wobbling on the top of his neck, and somehow it penetrated, it got down through the fog of the drugs, and he licked his lips and he was afraid.

In that moment, Greenberg knew. His eyes got as wide as saucers. He leaned forward.

"Tell! Tell me! Tell me what it is, and I'll make you rich beyond your wildest dreams! I'll take you away from all this! I'll keep you safe! I'll give you whatever you need!"

"It's not what you think," Gavin said dopily. "It won't ... it won't help you."

"For the love of God!" Greenberg cried. "Tell me what it is!"

His eyes glittered in his wrinkled face.

Gavin, fumbling, told him.

After they left, Gavin felt some regret, so he took another pill.

She was doing yoga in tight black pants and a pink tank top when she heard the bell ring. She paused, her feet spread apart, bent over with her hands on the ground. Then she straightened and walked over the door and peered through the peephole, and of course she let him in, because it was her brother.

Her boyfriend came to her apartment forty-five minutes later. He was the one who called the police. They didn't have any trouble finding Todd; he was across the street in an Arby's, sitting in a little plastic booth with her purse on the table and her bloody shirt balled up in one of his fists.

About two weeks later Gavin was sitting in the backyard In lawn chair made of sagging canvas stretched over a cracked metal frame. The headline in the newspaper caught his eye: ALLEGED MOBSTER MISSING - Millionaire Aaron Greenberg Still Missing After Leaving Hospital.

The past two weeks had gone by in a blur. The police, the funeral, all the people in the house. The drugs to lubricate it all. Nothing had really felt like it had gotten all the way in. Until this.

Gavin stared at the paper for a while. He read the article. Then he put the paper down and hauled himself to his feet. Using the crutches he made his way inside and took the car keys off the hook next to the fridge.

He wracked his memory on the way to the house, trying to remember the conversation with Greenberg. Parts of it were fuzzy, but most of it was etched with a strange, hallucinatory clarity. Like a vivid dream.

It was hot and humid. Gavin parked the car on the shoulder and hauled himself out of the car. Climbing the hill was one of the hardest things he'd ever done. The ground was moist and treacherous and hidden by the leaves and ferns and grass. Finally, after stumbling a few too many times, he lay on his belly and pulled himself up with his arms. Mosquitoes hummed in the air around his head, occasionally darting down to feed. Sometimes something bigger would rustle in the foliage. The muck got all up on Gavin's arms and his shirts. He was soaked with sweat. And all the time the house hung above him, solid and unmoving, ruined and magnificent, seeming to mock him somehow, and his trivial endeavours.

He switched back to crutches when he got to the top of the hill, limped to the front door and reached the door that led downstairs. The lock had been cut; it lay on the ground. The door was open.

Here was where he had to be careful; he watched his step on the way down. One step at a time. It also gave him a great excuse to stare at his feet instead of looking anywhere else. When he reached the bottom, the excuse was gone, and so he looked up.

The first thing he noticed was the circle of salt was empty. The second was the corpse at the far wall. Of course, he had smelt it on the way down. Flies were jumping on and off everything in sight, rubbing their little hands together with glee. Gavin lurched a couple of steps closer to the body just to confirm it was not Todd's buddy, the one who had been in the circle. It was Henry, his head twisted around 180 degrees, like the little girl in *The Exorcist*.

Something was written on the wall above the body, faint and jagged, in human blood, but it was too dark to make out what it was. He took a lighter out of his pocket and flicked it on and held it up to the wall and read the message, scrawled in a childlike hand in letters a foot high:

HE WANTED TO LIVE ANOTHER HUNDRED YEARS.

And although he didn't want to, although he wanted to do nothing more than to drag himself out of this dank and depressing basement that stunk of urine and stale marijuana, he lurched over towards the circle of salt.

Only it was not quite a circle any more. Someone had broken it, a small, messy cut, a few inches across. And next to this break there were two things – an empty pile of clothes, including a yarmaluke sitting on top like a cherry on a sundae, and an oxygen tank.

But the clothes weren't quite empty. Something was in there, something that was moving just a little bit. Something about the size and shape of a fireplace log. Gavin poked the clothing with the butt of one of his crutches for a while, stirring them around, and then suddenly a little pair of jaws slammed shut on the wood.

He tried to tell himself it wasn't Greenberg, but he couldn't.

Because of the eyes.

Mr. Marvin refused to come. Understandably. Gavin drove to Gainesville alone. He was off the painkillers, something that had seemed impossible only a few days ago, but they hadn't been able to make the vision of the basement disappear (the corpse, the writing, the empty circle, the thrashing baby crocodile) and so: what good were they, really? It was early enough that the withdrawal was more melancholy than painful; like a lover's last sigh, like the noise of the ocean withdrawing after the crash of a wave.

The prison was an ugly building but it didn't look like a prison. It was too functional. Prisons and police stations always look too much like regular buildings, like there was nothing special about them. He limped inside and they waved him through.

"Why do you want to see that loser?" the guard asked.

"I can see him though, right?" Gavin asked.

The guard, a heavyset functionary with a shaved head and little glasses, made a face.

"Yeah, you can see him. It was the only thing he asked for when he plead guilty."

"He asked for it?"

"Word is that he was expecting someone. Fucking creep."

It felt like there was something heavy on his shoulders.

They walked into the visitor's hall. The visitors were mainly black and Hispanic women. There was no drama or emotion. They stared at their men through the glass and spoke through the telephone. Some were forced and cheerful; others were complaining. The prisoners mostly listened, although some were agitated, spoke quickly and interrupted, argued or offered advice.

"He's got it pretty tough in here, I bet," Gavin said.

"I wish," the guard said. "No one fucking touches him. I don't know how he does it, the little shit. He probably creeps out the hard cases in here as much as everyone else. Shows you what a fucking piece of work he is."

Gavin sat down in his plastic chair and waited. He didn't wait long; after a few minutes Todd was led in, shuffling in his chains, a guard at his elbow.

Only it wasn't Todd; not even close. Not even a good imitation.

The demon sat down and looked at Gavin for a little while, smiling its sly smile, before it picked up the phone and spoke: "Hello."

Gavin's mouth opened. No sound came out.

"I knew you'd come," the demon said.

Silence.

"You don't have anything to say. That's okay," the demon said. It was using Todd's mouth, but it didn't even sound like him. "You likely don't even really know why you're here."

"Todd," Gavin said. Not believing the word he said.

The demon laughed. "If you want to talk to Todd, go ahead. He can hear you. I can even tell you what he says. I hear him quite well. I hear him screaming all the time."

"Todd," Gavin said. You did something wrong, but it's all right."

The demon looked to be growing bored.

"You're going to die soon, Todd," Gavin said. "Just give your heart over to God. And you'll be all right. I know you're not all bad."

"There is no God, you know," the demon said. "But there are other worlds than this. Oh yes. And there are things in them. Things like me. Things that are very big and very, very old, and well, very different from people like you. And normally, we can't get into this world, and we don't really want to. Because you people, well. You just come and go so quickly and you're very small and, frankly, the things you do just aren't very interesting. Every now and then, though, one of you, I don't know how to put this. Let's say, catches our eye, although, actually, we don't have eyes. And then, maybe, we see if there isn't something we can do. Because we are very old, and we live a long time. And every now and then it's good to, oh, say, shake things up, just a little."

Gavin put his head to his chest and he started to cry. It was not grief. Nor was he blaming himself for what had happened to Todd or Kristy or anyone else; he'd done that enough. It was just the universe, and how unfriendly it really seemed to be, when you got down to what its essential character. And how it really was too bad that it had to be that way.

"Your tears," the demon said in a slow, reflective voice. "We don't have anything like them. Nothing at all. You know, you people are very boring from far away. Because you are so small. But when you get close up, there just are so many little details."

Gavin hung up the phone. The demon knocked on the glass. Gavin couldn't hear what he was saying without the phone. Against his better judgment he picked the phone back up.

"If you're gonna threaten me, just save it, I get the picture."

"I wanted to tell you," the demon said. "That it's not over."

"What'd I just say?"

"I mean it's not too late for you. Remember what I said before? Even now. It's not too late. You won't be here too long, but you're here now. And although some doors have closed for you, closed forever, an infinite number still remain open. That's what it's like for your kind. I know that now. That's why you're different from us. So that's my gift to you, Gavin Rollins."

The demon smiled.

"Oh yes. I know your name. You don't know mine, but I know yours. I know your name, and know who you are. Little man with little worries. Because that's all they are. So don't you worry, and don't you cry. Now dry your eyes and have a safe drive home."

It was evening when his sponsor came to visit him, with the light shining slanted and amber through the waving leaves on the trees. The air was brisk and a little damp, presaging a rain, and as he had so many times since he'd spoken to the demon, Gavin felt like he was being watched.

"Hey there Gavin," his sponsor said.

Gavin twisted in his chair and looked behind him. His sponsor was named Phil; a little wiry man, a lawyer, a small town intellectual, well-read and lonely, who had drunk himself to sleep every night for years until he made some mistakes at work and gotten suspended and then drank so much he hadn't been able to sleep at all and he'd driven out in his old beige Cadillac with a bottle of Wild Turkey between his legs intending to kill himself but instead he'd suddenly found Jesus and joined AA and hadn't now had a drink in twelve years.

Gavin was the first man he'd sponsored.

"Hello," Gavin said.

"Mind if I join you?"

"Please do."

Gavin's sponsor sat down in the chair next to him.

"Where's the fellow you're staying with?"

"He's inside. He took to drink."

"Ah."

Phil did little nervous things with his hands. They crept around like spiders in his lap.

"You're sure this is the proper environment for you, then?"

"I'm all right."

"I was a little worried about the pain killers. I'm glad you seem to be in good shape. I hadn't seen you since you were in the hospital. You were as glassy-eyed as a doll. The painkillers can be really troublesome for recovering alcoholics."

"Yeah, they're something all right."

Phil looked at the book Gavin was holding. "How are you finding Faulkner?"

"Hard," Gavin said. "Look, I appreciate you coming out here and all, but I just want to be by myself."

"Yeah, I know," Phil said. "And I'll go, if you want me to. Because nothing good ever comes of forcing a man to go to a meeting. But Gavin, you need to get yourself to a meeting. It's not enough to not drink or not take pills. That doesn't mean you're not an alcoholic.

You're just dried out. That's all. There's only one cure that I know of. We got a meeting in twenty minutes in the church. Why don't you come with me? You don't have to say a word."

Inside the church the air was warm and dry and the sunset was spectacular through the west windows. They took the stairs at the back down into the basement where the light came from fluorescent bulbs that ran along the ceiling. There was a coffee machine and someone had brought a box of Arrowroot cookies. A dozen of the regulars were scattered through the room in the plastic chairs. Gavin and his sponsor sat down towards the back.

Towards the end of the evening, the man at the podium looked at Gavin and smiled.

"Do you have anything to say tonight, Gavin?"

"Gavin's fine," his sponsor said. "He's here to listen tonight."

"Come on Gavin," the man said. "We know you've got something to say. It can be anything."

Gavin smiled a little.

"It can't be anything," Gavin said.

"Sure it can," the man said. "Come on up and tell us. We're here for you. We'll listen."

"Never mind," Phil said. "Not tonight."

"Come on," the man said, and motioned up to the front again.

"No, no," Phil said, "he doesn't have to."

But Gavin was thinking. About that road, and how long it was, without any turning, and about how it didn't really lead anywhere at all. And how he could get up and leave the church but he wouldn't really be going anywhere. As he'd told Todd, there was no escape, there was no other world. This was it.

"It's all right, Phil," he said softly.

When he was up front, everyone watched him, their heads tilted back, smiling, nodding, encouraging.

"Hi everyone," he said. "My name's Gavin."

"Hello Gavin," everyone said.

"Uh, well, some of you know me. I see some new faces in here too. And that's really good. I haven't been here in a while. And, uh, it's good to be back."

Nodding.

"I haven't had a drink in fourteen months, but I don't know If I've been sober for that long. I was injured very badly two months ago.

And they gave me some, ah, some pretty neat pills. I wonder if anyone here maybe knows about them."

"Mmm-hmm," a few people said. Someone laughed.

"Anyway, that's all done with too," Gavin said. "So I stand before you a sober man."

A little wave of small cheers.

"I, uh. I don't know how to say this next part. I'm not even sure what I want to say."

Gavin looked away. He felt beaten, utterly and finally beaten.

"I, uh, I've made some decisions recently. Some mistakes. And it's hard for me to think what would have happened if I'd just ... if I'd just done them a little differently."

Gavin put his hands to his eyes for a moment.

"And I feel like I almost got something, something I really wanted and I really needed to have, you know? And then I lost it forever."

And for a little while Gavin cried, at the lectern in front of his fellow alcoholics, while they tutted like gentle hens and nodded and waited with maternal patience.

"But I feel, I don't know, I feel like I learned so much. I feel like I learned about myself. And you know, maybe that's something. I'd give that knowledge back, if I could, to turn things back to how they used to be before. But I can't make that trade, no matter how much I want to. So I have to let it go. And I realized, I think, that maybe that's what it's been all along. Letting go. Just as simple as that. There's so many things in my life, so many feelings, about myself. And all the time it's been me holding on to them. I don't know why; I don't know why.

"And I've learned that, and now I need to do it. Now I need to do it more than ever. And I realize, that knowing I need to do it, and actually doing it, are two different things. I wonder if I even deserve to do it. I wonder if I even deserve to ... move on ... or if I should stay here forever. Because maybe that's what I deserve. To stay in this spot forever. Trapped by something so small."

Gavin cried harder.

"But I can move on. Even if I don't deserve to. I guess that I can. I guess you can beat anything in life, as long as you know its name."

6 Butler to the fairies

As a boy, Stephen was a lout. His hair was dark and unkempt, he had a prominent brow, and the lower part of his face was fixed in a perpetual frown. He was big-boned and uncouth and did not do well in school. In this he was very much unlike his father, Martin, and the two of them did not at all get on. Martin considered Stephen to be a disappointment. Stephen, for his part, held his father in contempt, particularly on account of his profession. Stephen was keenly embarrassed to be the son of the village cunning man.

Martin's second son was named Chester, and he was everything Stephen was not. He was graceful, almost feminine, in his movements, and his build was delicate. His features were fine and his hair was fair. He was a cheerful boy and good at school.

Considering the way that Martin openly favoured Chester, one might expect that Stephen would have resented his little brother. And certainly, Stephen would cuff Chester over the head and threaten to throw his books into the well.

But a careful observer might have noted that Stephen never actually cuffed Chester all that hard, and nor did he ever carry out his threats. Chester, for his part, idealized his older brother, and the two of them often spent their free hours roaming through the gentle fields and hills of the Yorkshire Dales.

On one sunny afternoon while they were (at Chester's instigation) collecting different kinds of insects in a glass jar, they encountered their father's hired man, Mr. Grandyfellow. Mr. Grandyfellow was shorter than average and very thin. His skin was pale and his features were pinched, which gave him a slightly murine appearance. The most unusual thing about him was that he never opened his mouth when he smiled (which he often did, for he was a very jolly fellow).

"Hello!" he called to them. "Hello!"

Stephen and Martin were walking along a narrow country road when they heard his voice. Mr. Grandyfellow was about a hundred yards away, halfway up an ashy limestone hill. He was wearing a neat grey suit and waving at them with both hands. There was a large basket next to him.

"What's he want?" Stephen asked.

"Hello there!" Mr. Grandyfellow called. "Come on over here! I've got something for you!"

Chester looked at Stephen.

"Let's just leave," Chester said.

"No," Stephen said. "Let's go see him."

"I don't like him."

"I don't like him either," Stephen said. "He's a poof. But let's go see what he's got. He can't hurt us."

Chester didn't look very sure about that, but Stephen was already climbing over the loose stone wall, and Chester had no choice but to follow, carrying his little jar of bugs in his hand.

"Hello there boys!" Mr. Grandyfellow said as they approached. "What a coincidence! How very nice to see you!"

He was smiling with his mouth tightly shut.

The boys didn't say anything.

"I was just about to have a picnic," Mr. Grandyfellow said, "and I was hoping you would both join me."

At the world picnic Chester jerked and looked at Stephen. Their father had warned them about Mr. Grandyfellow, as he often warned them against his servants, associates and companions. In particular, Martin had told the boys many times, very sternly, that they must never eat or drink anything Mr. Grandyfellow might offer them.

Stephen ignored his brother.

"What have you got?" he asked.

The basket opened, and out came a roast chicken, cookies and crackers, a thermos of hot chocolate, some cheese wrapped in wax paper, grapes, oranges, a bag of nuts, and many other things that were good to eat. Indeed, so much food came out, so quickly, that it was difficult to understand how there had been room for it all in there.

"Please," Mr. Grandyfellow said. "Help yourselves! There's more than enough for everyone."

"No thank you," Chester said.

"Oh, no, please, do help yourself," Mr. Grandyfellow said, smiling his closed-mouth smile. "Please! You must be hungry. You're frightfully hungry! I can tell."

"No," Chester said. "Come on, Stephen. Let's go back to the road."

"Why?" Stephen said. He was looking at a ham sandwich. "Why shouldn't we? I'm hungry."

And then he sat down and took up a sandwich and began to eat it.

Chester looked miserable but Stephen returned his gaze stonily, without any emotion at all.

"There!" Mr. Grandyfellow cried, the corners of his mouth jerking upward but his lips staying firmly pressed together. "Isn't it nice? Isn't that a nice sandwich?"

Stephen munched away. In later years he would honestly not be able to remember what he had been thinking in these moments, what he had been trying to prove, and to whom. He would search his soul for answers, attempting, in all honesty, to recall if he had perceived any danger or if he had harboured any ill-will to his brother. But he would never be able to remember. In his mind's eye he would always be able to see himself, sitting on the rocky hillside, eating the ham sandwich, but it was always as if he was looking upon a stranger, someone whose inner workings were a mystery to him.

"Are you sure you won't join us?" Mr. Grandyfellow said. He sat down, carefully folding his thin legs underneath him, and began to nibble on a scone. "You're certain I can't tempt you with anything?"

Chester didn't say anything. By this time, Stephen had finished his sandwich and was moving on to a drumstick.

"You're such a coward, Chester," Stephen said. "You always were."

And how Chester's face fell, at those words, how miserable he looked.

"Now Stephen," Mr. Grandyfellow said, "that's no way to talk to your brother."

Trying not to weep, Chester sat down next to Stephen.

"Please, let's go."

"Why are you so afraid?" Stephen said. "Why do you have to do everything father tells you?"

"I'm not hungry."

"Well I am, so you can take your silly bugs and go home if you don't want anything."

Stephen kept munching, even though he, in truth, was not all that hungry, and the food from the basket had a funny dusty aftertaste.

"If I eat something, can we go?" Chester asked.

"Fine," Stephen said.

Chester sat down and picked up bun. He raised it to his mouth and took a few bites miserably.

"There," Mr. Grandyfellow said. "Not so bad, is it?"

He put his hand on Chester's shoulder and smiled, but this time he opened his mouth. Chester didn't notice, because he was looking at Stephen, but Stephen did. Mr. Grandyfellow had too many teeth. They were not large or pointed. There were just too many of them. Far too many. And for just a moment, there was a flicker of colour in Mr. Grandyfellow's eyes, as if they had suddenly turned pitch black, as if a dark shade had been dropped and lifted.

Stephen made a screeching noise, scrambled to his feet, and then turned and fled. He had not formed any conscious desire to abandon his brother. His body had simply reacted. A shriek came from behind him, and then a terrible laugh, high and silvery, like the tinkling of little bells.

"Stephen!" his brother screamed, but his cry was silenced partway through, as if it had been cut off by a slamming door.

Stephen leapt over the wall and tried to run down the road, but then Mr. Grandyfellow shouted out a string of words in a foreign language, and Stephen fell to the ground, feeling as if all of his muscles had gone to sleep. There was nothing he could do but lie still and listen to the sound of Mr. Grandyfellow's light footsteps approaching.

But he also heard a different sound, that of the engine of a motor car coming up the road. Stephen's heart beat frantically in his chest while he waited for a hand to fall on his back, but that hand never came. Instead the motor car drove up to him and stopped, and Stephen found that the strength in his limbs had returned, and he could get back to his feet.

They never found any sign of Chester, Mr. Grandyfellow, the food or the picnic basket. They never found anything except the little glass jar, with all the imprisoned bugs inside, clambering over one another.

Martin had the whole story out of Stephen, and then knocked him down and shouted at him, cursing him for a fool, before he retreated into his study to consult his books. Martin tried every spell he knew. He was at it for weeks. Nothing worked.

Afterwards, they rarely spoke, and eventually Stephen ran away to London.

The English countryside went into a steep decline after the war, but it began to rebound under Thatcher. Not that things got any better for ordinary people; at least, not at first. But a new generation of young rich people rose up in City and began to snap up country estates. At first Lloyd Luxton was suspicious of these newcomers, but he grew to appreciate them. They pushed up the value of his estate, which had sagged disastrously under Wilson. More importantly, since Luxton was himself one of the few authentic old aristocrats in the area, one of the few surviving remnants of an era this new generation could imitate but never join, they demonstrated a rather pathetic willingness to sit at his table, drink his mediocre port, and listen attentively to his tales of what things used to be like in the old days.

In particular, they admired his old butler, Stephen, a tall, powerfully-built, silver-haired fellow with an indescribably authentic air. It was not that he was particularly sophisticated, because he wasn't. The slick servants these bank managers and publishing magnates brought up from London were far more knowledgeable about gourmet foods and elaborate table settings that Stephen was, or could ever hope to be. Nor was it that he was charming or witty. However he possessed a quality which more accomplished servants lacked.

There is probably no precise word for this quality, and so the simple term 'dignity' will have to suffice. Stephen was dignified without being ponderous or stuffy. He was quiet and diligent without being stupid, principled but unpretentious. In a crisis he was calm and calmed those around him. Simply by existing he made the ground under your feet feel more solid. Looking at Stephen, you couldn't help but feel that the universe was an orderly place with discernible rules, and that you would get along all right if you would just part your hair neatly and keep a stiff upper lip. Drunken partygoers lowered their voice in his presence without feeling unduly intimidated, and children appealed to him when they disagreed over the rules of their games.

Mr. Luxton often had visitors during the summer. The manor house was, to be honest, a little unpleasant in the winter months. A damp cold seemed to leach through the walls and the entire west wing was closed down for the season. But in the summer the whole property was lovely, with rolling fields fenced in by ancient stone walls, which were pleasantly overgrown without actually being wild. On this particular weekend he was being visited by a middle-aged Canadian named Professor Harwood. Harwood was a stooping, obsequious man with very weak blue eyes and pale orange hair.

"I knew his father," Luxton said while he was eating his breakfast in bed. "He owned a hog-processing plant in Toronto. One of those dreadful mechanized places where they turn a pig into eight different kinds of produce in under a half an hour, and where they waste no part of the animal, if you take my meaning. But he made a packet off it, enough to set up his idiot son at York University. I take it he is a professor of witchcraft, or some such humbug."

"I see, sir," Stephen said.

"Got the most amusing letter from him," Luxton said. "Apparently he's coming up here to take a look at some old books that used to belong to a fellow named Martin Moore. No relation of yours, I take it?"

"No sir," Stephen said.

"I shouldn't think so," Luxton said. "Well, Stephen, we must endure a dreadful bore like this once every two months or so to ensure we have material for conversations with our less preposterous visitors. Don't you agree?"

"If you say so, sir," Stephen said. "I'll have the green room aired out."

Stephen carried down the tray to the kitchen. The cook, a hardened red-faced woman who had worked for Luxton for years, was much attuned to Stephen's moods, and noticed that there was something a little off with him. But she knew better than to bother to ask.

The visitors arrived by train at 2:10 pm on Saturday. Stephen spent the morning cleaning Lloyd's Rolls Royce, inside and out, applying a tooth brush to the smallest crevasses, and then drove to the station pick them up.

It was a beautiful day. A large number of people were coming off the train. Many of them looked like day-trippers from the City, small, wide, loud people who wiped their mouths with the back of their hands and were surrounded by boisterous mobs of children. They parted around Stephen like the sea.

Professor Harwood was not easily distinguishable from the masses, but his servant certainly was. She was a tall black woman, stooped and thin, with grey braided hair and clever eyes. She looked around her with frank curiosity. A little girl was tagging behind at her side, dressed in an old-fashioned dress, and prettier than her mother.

Once Stephen spotted them, it was easy to spot the professor, a graying, heavyset man with damp, loosely curled hair and thick glasses. Stephen raised one finger to them and they made their way over.

The professor was not a light packer; he had brought many heavy chests filled with books. It was necessary to hire a taxi to bring over the servant, the girl and the luggage. The professor rode in the back of the Rolls Royce, and spent the entire trip reading, without once speaking to Stephen or looking out the window.

When they returned to the manor Stephen showed the professor to his room. They still did not have a large staff, and so it was left to Stephen and his skinny under-butler Reginald to carry the trunks of books upstairs. Afterwards, the professor stayed in his room to get ready for dinner while Stephen went downstairs to find the servant.

She was in the kitchen, unpacking her own bags, which contained her own cast iron cookware as well as a variety of small packages of spice.

"Oh, hello Mr. Stephen," she said. "I been talking to your cook here. I hope you'll tell her it's all right if I just put my things here."

The cook, who was so flustered by this unexpected intrusion she was barely angry, implored to Stephen to protect her domain.

"I must say, madam," Stephen began.

"You can call me Miss Stacey."

"Miss Stacey," Stephen said, "our cook is very particular about her kitchen."

"Oh, yes sir," Miss Stacey said, beaming.

"And she is in the midst of preparing for dinner."

"Oh yes, Mr. Stephen," Stacey said. "I can see that sir."

"And indeed she has prepared a menu for the whole weekend."

"Oh, no sir!" Stacey said. "The whole weekend? Not the whole weekend. That ain't right. You just let me know where to put my things and then I'll take care of lunch tomorrow. Mr. Stephen, please. You'll make me ashamed of myself."

Something in this appeal touched Stephen's own ideal of service. The dignity of it. And so, he gave a sympathetic glance to the cook, who reluctantly ceded some territory in the corner.

That night at dinner Lloyd got very drunk and made a lot of jokes about the Cottingley Fairies. The professor lowered his head into his collar like a turtle and stammered and sweated. Stephen tactfully interrupted the conversation by offering food or drink whenever things got too unpleasant.

After dinner Stephen told Stacey:

"You know Miss Stacey, when Mr. Luxton has gentlemen visitors, I usually invite the butler for a sherry in the servant's common area. Since the Professor does not have a butler, you'd be welcome to join me tonight."

"Oh, thank you sir!" Miss Stacey said. "I'd be glad to."

After the plates were washed, and the silverware was polished and counted and locked back in the cabinet, Stephen made a quick round to speak with the other servants and then headed down into the servant's common area. He loosened his tie and took the sherry out of the cupboard and sat down in the armchair next to the fire. As he was carefully packing the tobacco in his pipe, a little head peeped around the corner to the door.

Stephen looked at the child for a moment, and then waggled his eyebrows comically. The child's eyes crinkled with humour.

"Jessi!" Stacey's voice shouted out. "Don't make me come find you!"

Stacey came into the common room, looked around at the humble table, the fox hunting watercolour hanging from the walls, and at Stephen sitting in his chair.

"Mr. Stephen, have you seen my little girl anywhere around here?" she asked.

"I'm sorry, Miss Stacey," he said. "Would you like any help looking for her?"

"Oh, she'll turn up," Miss Stacey said darkly, and wandered back into the hall. When she returned five minutes later to ask Stephen a question, she was shocked to see her daughter, Jessica, standing at Stephen's feet and taking short puffs of smoke from his pipe.

"Jessi!" she shrieked. "You put that down! Mr. Stephen, I'm surprised at you! Given tobacco to a little girl like that! Jessi, you come over here right this instant!"

And Jessi did just that, skipping into her mother's arm with the confidence of a child that had never been struck. Stacey ushered her away, still nagging away in her high, loud voice, while Stephen carefully cleaned off the nub of his pipe with his handkerchief, his expression inscrutable.

When Stacey returned she took a seat and accepted a glass of sherry and made no mention of the smoking incident. Instead she said:

"Well Mr. Stephen, your employer is just about the rudest man I ever seen. Why it was terrible to see the way he was teasing the professor about his fairies."

"Mr. Luxton can be very frank in his opinions," Stephen said. "Have you worked for the professor long?"

"Only my whole life, that's all," Stacey said. "He was born when I was seven years old. I held him when he was a little baby. He was so happy when he was young. But his father, Old Mr. Harwood, well, he was just a bully, and nothing the professor could do was ever good enough for him. I suppose it is a little silly to be a professor of fairies but he don't hurt no one and his last book sold a lot of copies, he said."

"I'm sure," Stephen said, "that he's a leader in his field."

"Anyway," Stacey said. "He's been looking forward to this trip the whole time, but the food here don't agree with him. I ain't never been to England before. The furthest I've ever been is down to Jamaica to see my cousin. I brought my daughter for her education. I didn't have the opportunity to travel. My mamma did her best for me but those were different days when I was younger and she never did much for my education. Things will be different for Jessi. Yes sir. She's getting a European tour before she turns ten years old. Mmm-hmm."

Stacey sipped the sherry.

"Hmm! This is real nice. I only ever had cooking sherry before."

"Yes," Stephen said. "I keep this bottle aside for special occasions."

"Why thank you, Mr. Stephen. I hope you'll come to Canada one day to visit us. Have you ever been to Canada?"

"No."

"Have you travelled much?"

"I've accompanied Mr. Lloyd around Europe," Stephen said.

"What was your favourite?"

"The south of France is rather nice," Stephen said. "Indeed, it has many advantages over the north of England. The food, the climate. The sea is as warm as a bathtub. Still, although I confess I could never explain why, I would never want to leave here. This is my home."

"Well, that's just what home is, Mr. Stephen," Stacey said, and sipped her port. "Still, you can't be too tied to your home. I've known folks like that. They don't want to let things go."

Stephen smiled and smoked his pipe.

"Tell me, Miss Stacey, have you ever seen a fairy?"

"Mr. Stephen, now, don't you start."

"I'm serious. You've never seen your employer do any magic, have you?"

"No, of course not," Stacey said. "No fairies, goblins, witches, no nothing like that."

"What about the professor's colleagues?"

"What about them?"

"You haven't seen them do any magic, have you?"

"Mr. Stephen, I'm surprised at you again. I didn't think I'd hear this from you. There's no such thing as magic."

"And he doesn't have any strange friends? Or servants?"

"All his friends are strange. They're strange old fuddy-duddies who never married and try to talk to their dead pets with Ouija boards. Don't lets talk bad about the professor. He was a happy little baby and he's like a little brother to me. One day he'll maybe send my Jessi to college. He don't know any magic but he won't hurt anyone neither."

"I hope not, Miss Stacey," Stephen said, and smiled. "Would you care for another glass of sherry?"

The professor left quite early in the morning. Reginald was driving him to the local archives and library, as well as to the homes of a number of venerable residents of the town who had collected old books and other antiques. He returned just in time for lunch, a spicy seafood boil prepared by Stacey. The regular cook claimed that the dish lacked subtlety, but Lloyd greatly enjoyed it. He smacked his lips over each spoonful and said: "It's a rare dish that can cut through the film of old age. Your cook, professor, is welcome to visit any time."

That night the professor took his dinner in his room.

"You don't suppose I was too hard him, do you?" Lloyd said as he tucked into a plate of hushpuppies and chicken fried steak.

"No sir," Stephen said. "Men must be prepared to defend their beliefs."

Through the day the little girl, Jessica, had explored the grounds; picking through the brambles, climbing the stone walls, poking around inside the barn, throwing rocks into the barn. She had a large dinner of leftovers down in the servants' quarters with Stephen and Stacey, laughing and showing her white teeth. That night Stephen awoke in a sweat just after midnight, his whole body tingling painfully with pins and needles. A sound like the gentle ringing of tiny bells was in the air. In the morning Jessica was gone.

As you might imagine, the whole household was frantic. Stacey was dreadfully worried, and although she had enough self-control to avoid totally dissolving into hysterics, it was plain to everyone how devastated she was. Her voice was high and squeaky and tears would leak out of the corners of her eyes when she spoke. The other servants were very sympathetic and organized into little bands that searched the town. Even Lloyd was personally concerned, allowing his motorcars to transport people to spread the alarm.

The only one who was absent was the professor. He spent most of the day in his room. Around lunchtime he came downstairs for his lunch, but since everyone was out searching for the little girl, nothing was prepared. And so he just hung around the edges, watching everyone hurry back and forth, with a peculiar fixed expression on his face, before he headed back upstairs.

No one paid much attention to him, except for Stephen, who watched the professor carefully, albeit with very little outward display of emotion.

A few minutes later, Stephen had a brief conversation with Reginald regarding the meals for the searchers, and then, left alone, he ascended the broad curling staircase up to the second floor, the heavy tread softly clumping through the carpet. He came to the professor's door, and knocked.

"Go away," the professor said. "I'm busy."

Stephen knocked again.

"I said go away!"

He knocked a third time.

The door opened.

"Are you deaf?" the professor said. "I'd like to be left alone."

The room smelt very close. The windows were closed and the shades were drawn and books were scattered all over the floor. Stephen glanced inside for the barest of moments and then he flicked his eyes to the professor's face.

"What do you want?" the professor said.

Stephen did not say anything. He stood there, a tall, powerful elderly man, ungraceful, dignified, and looked the professor right in the eye.

"I asked you what do you want?" the professor said.

Stephen remained silent. The professor then looked down.

"I don't know what you think," the professor said, and started mopping his forehead with the back of his sleeve. "I don't ..." He trailed off, and then coughed.

Stephen waited a little longer, and then he spoke:

"Was it a very thin man? Ratty-looking? Too many teeth?"

The professor looked startled. "How did you ..." he began.

The lines around Stephen's eyes and mouth began to harden.

"I didn't do anything!" the professor said. "I didn't! The girl was hiding outside my room, and he was the one who saw her! He just offered her something to eat, and I didn't see the harm in it! It's not my fault!"

Silence from the butler.

"It isn't!" the professor said. "It isn't!"

Stephen did not say anything. He did not seem hurried in the least. And eventually the professor started staring back down at the ground.

"Well, I ... I ..."

"I think you should make preparations to summon our mutual friend again this evening, sir," Stephen said.

"I have!" the professor said. "Good lord man! What do you think I've been doing all day, hmm? I can't make him come!"

"Oh, I rather think you can sir," Stephen said. "If you can make him come once, you can make him come again. What you can't do, I'm afraid, is make him visible once you've brought him to you. You will leave that to me."

"What?" the professor said. "Do you know magic?"

"Oh no sir," Stephen said. "I'm only the butler. Good evening sir."

He went downstairs, nodding to the servants he passed, and made his way into the dining room. It caused him no small pain to do it, but he unlocked the cabinet and scooped up the silverware and dumped it into a cloth bag. All of the slick, cold beautiful utensils that he had so many times held in his hands, turning them critically backwards and forwards under the light while some maid anxiously twisted her apron in her hands, awaiting his verdict on her work. All for naught. Ah well. Omnia mutantor, nihil interdit, as the ancients said.

Evening came and Stephen knocked on the professor's door. After a few moments of shuffling, the door opened, and Stephen came inside.

"Would you be so good as to open the windows, sir?" Stephen asked.

"Why is that?" the professor asked. "Something about the sunset?"

"My good sir," Stephen said, "as far as I know, fairies are quite indifferent to the weather. But, if I am to be totally truthful, I must admit, it is rather oppressive in here."

And so they opened the windows, one after another, and let the clean night air in. For a moment Stephen stood and admired the view, his hand resting on the sill above his head, and wondered how country side which looked so manicured and tame could contains creatures of such all-surpassing wildness.

He cleared a place in a steep-backed leather chair by putting the books stacked there on the floor, and rested his arm on the table.

"You may proceed sir," Stephen said.

"Are you sure?" the professor said.

"Quite."

The professor shrugged irritably and then drew up his sleeves. A great leather tome, which looked quite familiar to Stephen, was set up on a lectern, and the professor read from it in a clear and confident voice, sounding very practiced. The spell did not take long. Nothing happened. The professor ran his hands through his hair and looked at Stephen.

"I *told* you so," he began.

"Mr. Grandyfellow," Stephen said. "Do you remember me?"

And the fairy suddenly winked into view, not far from the professor, who gave a cry and started so hard he almost fell over.

"Do I?" Mr. Grandyfellow said, smiling his tight-lipped smile. "Do I remember you, Stephen? Why yes! Yes I do!"

The professor ran over to one side of the room and began rooting through a bag he had on the floor.

"I remember that you feasted with King Oberon," Mr. Grandyfellow said. "Oh, you didn't know it at the time, did you? But you ate at his table nevertheless. And that means there are certain obligations incumbent upon you, my good man, however hideous and wrinkled you've become. Yes! How wonderful it is, young master Stephen, to see you finally come good."

Stephen sat in his seat, erect, dignified.

"I am prepared to come with you," Stephen said, "upon the condition that ..."

"The condition!" Mr. Grandyfellow crowed, opening his mouth, and throwing his head back, so that Stephen could look on those rows and rows of straight, neat, white teeth. "Oh, Stephen, my dear young boy! The condition! The condition!"

The professor popped up from his bag and started rushing towards Mr. Grandyfellow wielding a garland of rowan and herbs. The fairy traced a single letter in the air and the professor tumbled onto the ground, fast asleep.

"Now where were we?" Mr. Grandyfellow said. "Oh yes!"

He made another gesture, and Stephen's head fell back against his chair, slack, with his mouth opened.

"You were coming with me," Mr. Grandyfellow said, "to serve King Oberon for a thousand years and a day!"

The fairy's grin spread across his face quickly, like a crack suddenly appearing in piece of wood that had been under strain for a long time. With two great, airy steps he crossed the distance to Stephen and grasped him by the wrist.

And so confident Mr. Grandyfellow was, so unprepared for any trickery from an elderly English butler, that the cold iron dagger had smashed through the back of his hand into the table before he could smell the horseshoe hanging around Stephen's neck.

There was a moment of silence, and then Mr. Grandyfellow began to shriek.

"Eeeeyahhh! Eeeeeyahhh!"

Stephen stood up slowly, and began taking some metallic objects out of his pockets.

"Take it out!" Mr. Grandyfellow screamed. "Ahhh! It burns! Ahhh!"

"Certainly," Stephen said. "Simply swear an oath to serve me."

"Serve you!" Mr. Grandyfellow hissed, while he bared his rows of teeth and narrowed his solid black eyes to slits. "Me, to serve you, after you ate our food? Never!"

"You know," Stephen said, "I was rather hoping you were going to say that."

And he raised his fists, which, Mr. Grandyfellow noticed with an overwhelming sense of alarm, were now clad with thick cold iron rings.

Stephen lifted his hands to his fists. In another life, a long time ago, he had tried to make his living as a boxer. He had never amounted to much, but he had not been without a small and vocal set of supporters. For what he had lacked in speed and skill, he had come very close to making up for with dogged mercilessness.

After two punches the fairy dropped to its knees and begged for mercy.

"I will serve you!" Mr. Grandyfellow said. "I will serve you! I swear it!"

"In all things, for all time, commencing now?" Stephen said.

"Yes!"

"And you shall come when I call you?"

"Yes!"

"And you shall not leave my side unless I give you permission?"

"Yes!"

"Very well," Stephen said.

He took the slender chain out of his pocket. Although the chain was made of cold iron, it had been coated in silver. Stephen snapped one end of it onto Grandyfellow's wrist, and wrapped the other one around his neck.

"What are you doing?" Mr. Grandyfellow said.

Stephen told him.

Mr. Grandyfellow's eyes, black as marbles, snapped open as wide as they could go.

"Oh no!" Mr. Grandyfellow. "You can't!"

"I can but try," Stephen said.

"No, no, no!" Mr. Grandyfellow screamed.

"Mr. Grandyfellow," Stephen said, as he jerked the knife out of the table, "I must remind you of your oath."

It is a well-known fact that fairies scarcely, if ever, visit this world any longer, so that many no longer even believe in their existence. Few people know why.

The general public believe (with, one suspects, the tacit approval and encouragement of the fairies themselves) that the fairies have left us because we have turned our back on them through technology. The general argument runs thus: once man was closely connected to nature, and understood the wind and trees and felt the pulse of mystical spirits in our veins. Now we are only concerned with television and fast food, and despoil the environment, and have no interest in magic, but only drab and pragmatic science.

The truth is altogether simpler. Fairies long regarded humans as their stupid, oafish, and feeble cousins. They were far more talented than us in the complex arts of magic, and so it was great sport for them to torment us. While no fairies are wholly evil, none of them are particularly good, and they do not regard us as worthy of any moral concern.

But, although magic is a wondrous thing, it is not, as the foolish believe, a limitless force, even if its limits are ill-defined and misunderstood. It is not, most importantly, a certain guarantee against technology. And so the fairies were first slightly alarmed by the arrival of the Romans, with their running water and military organization, then quite concerned by the development of gunfire, and then terrified by the detonation of the atom bomb.

The fairies did not leave this world because we turned our backs on magic, but because we became too powerful for them to pick on with safety. That's all there is to it.

It is always dusk in the world of the fairies; just a few minutes after the sun has set, so the sky to the west is all bruised and lit up, glowing, like a torch shining behind a dark blue blanket. The moon hangs low and fat in the sky, visible in slices through the sharp and slender branches. The trees are taller and the air is queerly still. There is none of the omnipresent noise of a natural forest; the birds, the bees, the crickets are all gone. Silence reigns, save for a whispering noise that echoes through the trees and singing that comes from very far away.

"Please," Mr. Grandyfellow said. "I don't think you know just what he'll do to us!"

"Hmm," Stephen said.

"For instance," Mr. Grandyfellow whispered, as he rubbed at the skin underneath the iron bracelet on his wrist. "I think you should know that nothing ever dies here! It's true! And so, death really isn't the worst thing. Really! And it isn't that Oberon will stay angry with you! Because he won't. But he'll forget about you. Do you understand? He will get very angry with us, and he will do something very dreadful, and then he will forget about us, forever."

"Mr. Grandyfellow," Stephen said. "I would be grateful if you would keep walking."

And the fairy did so, with a miserable look on his face that made it plain he was not in control of his limbs.

"But sir!" Mr. Grandyfellow exclaimed. "He'll do terrible things to them, too!"

"To whom are you referring?"

"The children, sir!" Mr. Grandyfellow said.

"I see. Your interest in their welfare is most touching."

"They don't have it that badly now," Mr. Grandyfellow said. "You don't know how much worse it can be for them!"

"I command you to be silent," Stephen said, "until I ask you to speak."

And he was.

The road they were on was very broad, but the course it ran was particularly winding, and the branches reached over their head to form a canopy that mostly blocked out the stars. Only the smiling moon was visible, every now and then, flickering through the gaps in the leaves and casting a silvery light on the cobblestones.

Whisper, whisper, whisper. A sound that was not the wind. More like the trees moving, subtly, imperceptibly. As they continued down the path, that sound, and the sound of their footsteps, was joined by eerie music, with long, tremulous notes that rose and fell quickly and smoothly. Mr. Grandyfellow rubbed the skin on his wrist and whined, but Stephen took no note of him.

Eventually the road widened into a large clearing, and the music became loud enough that it drowned out the little murmurs of the forest. The stars were in all the wrong places in the sky, and the face in the moon seemed darker and more pronounced than it did in the world of men. Tall, bare trees dotted the landscape, and in the distance a crumbling castle loomed against the glowing sky.

Mr. Grandyfellow was hopping from one foot to another and desperately pointing at his mouth.

"No," Stephen said.

On a tree near the castle a man was dangling by his heels. A glittering golden hook had been pushed through the flesh between his ankle bone and his Achilles tendon, and his body was covered with lashes and bite marks from small mouths. For a while Stephen stood at the foot of that tree and looked at the hanging man, and the hanging man looked back at him with faded grey eyes that seemed older than the universe.

"Who are you?" Stephen asked.

The man hesitated a moment, and then said:

"I do not remember."

The music grew louder, unpleasantly so, as they walked down the shimmering white path (it appeared to be made of mother of pearl) that lead to the front door of the castle. It made an almost painful sensation as it entered the ear, a vibration that set the teeth on edge, that got too far in. Like a screwdriver turning round, digging deeper. And Stephen could hear voices now, all speaking at once, chattering, like a great crowd, as well as the sound of hundreds of feet tramping on the wooden floor boards, making it bounce and squeak.

"Where are the children?" Stephen said.

Mr. Grandyfellow didn't say anything.

"You may speak."

"They're in the galley," Grandyfellow said. "There's a side door around the back. But sir ..."

"Please be silent," Stephen said.

They stepped off the path onto the damp earth. Green vines ran up and down the crumbling stone walls of the castle, which were so pitted and eroded that they looked like cheese. The air smelt like flowers. The noise from the party was overwhelming.

The side door was locked, but Mr. Grandyfellow opened it with a small golden key. Inside the galley was long and narrow, with counters on either side. Bronze oil lamps dangling from the ceiling lit up the room, but shadows lay in still pools in the corners. Cracks and chips dotted the paint on the walls.

Dirty dishes were stacked everywhere, piled on top of each other, canted this way and that, caked in chocolate and pea soup and other sticky material. And the children, a great horde of them, were washing frantically, up to their elbows in soapy water. None of them sniffled or cried. They seemed dazed rather than dismayed.

"Good heavens," Stephen said softly.

Jessica, the only black, was easy to spot, and Stephen walked over to where she was attacking the inside of a vile cast iron pot.

"Jessica."

The girl looked up at him with wide, startled eyes.

"Jessica."

"Yes?"

"Do you remember me?" he said as he knelt down beside her.

"Yes, you're Stephen."

"Are you all right?"

"Yes, I just have to finish these dishes. There's an awful lot of them. I think it will take me all night."

"Do you remember when you came here?"

"Yes, just last night," she said. "The man with you brought me here. Mr. Grandyfellow. He's the professor's friend. He said I could go back tomorrow morning when these dishes were finished."

"All right," Stephen said. "The only way for you to leave this place is to follow the white path into the dark woods. Once you're there, you'll eventually come to the door that brought us here. We left it open behind us. Do you understand?"

"Dark path," Jessica said, "white woods."

"No, no, child," Stephen said. "White path, dark woods."

"White path to the dark woods," Jessica said, very slowly, as if she had just woken up, or would shortly fall asleep.

"Wait for the music to stop," Stephen said. "When the music stops, you must run out the door, and then find the white path."

"All right, Stephen," Jessica said. "But you know, the music isn't ever going to stop."

"We shall see," Stephen said. He started to stand up, his stiff old knees creaking, and then he stopped. A little further down the line of children, working away at an enormous skillet, was Chester, his brother, looking no different from how he had on the day of his disappearance, almost fifty years before. Washing a skillet.

"Chester?" Stephen said.

The boy glanced at him and then looked back to his work.

Stephen put a shaking hand on his brother's shoulder.

"Chester?"

The boy looked up. His eyes were dull and exhausted.

"Yes?"

"Is it you?"

"Yes," Chester said. "I think so."

"Do you know me?"

"No, sir," Chester said. But then he blinked, focused his eyes a little, and added: "But you look like my father."

Stephen's chin trembled, for just a moment.

"Are you all right?"

"Yes sir," the boy said. "I just need to finish these dishes. I don't think we'll be done till the morning. It's like to take us all night."

Stephen was quiet for a moment.

"Do you remember how long you've been here?"

"I was just brought here last night," Chester said.

Chester looked past Stephen at Mr. Grandyfellow.

"He brought me here. He said I could go back tomorrow, once I'd finished the dishes."

"I see," Stephen said, looking around the room. "I see. Well, Chester, you listen to me. In a little while the music will stop."

"Oh no, sir," Chester said dully. "I don't think so."

"Yes it will. And when it does, you need to run out of this galley with all the little children. Find the white path in front of the castle, and follow it to the dark woods. You will come to a door. Go through it, bring all the children after you. And then shut the door behind you."

"All right sir," Chester said. "If you say so."

"I do, Chester. And Chester ..."

"Yes?"

"Do you remember your brother, Stephen?"

And then something happened that almost cracked Stephen's dignified mask, his shell, the shield he'd been building up his whole life.

Chester's face lit up with recognition.

"Yes, of course," he said. "Of course I know my brother."

Almost cracked it, but almost doesn't count. Stephen took a breath and steadied himself and carried on.

"You know," he said, "Stephen is dreadfully sorry for what happened to you."

"What do you mean?"

"That you were brought here."

"Really?"

"Yes. In fact, he was terribly guilty. He wanted me to tell you how sorry he was."

Chester smiled. "That's too bad," he said. "It wasn't his fault. Anyway, I'll see him tomorrow when I finish these dishes."

"Remember what I said about the music," Stephen said.

Chester nodded, his eyes starting to lose their focus.

"Right," he said. "Dark path, white forest."

And just as Stephen was turning back to Mr. Grandyfellow, the door to the galley banged upon and two fairies, short and slender and dressed in shimmering robes the same colour as the mother of pearl path, entered the galley and dumped armloads of dirty dishes.

One of the fairies, with blue hair and wide green eyes, saw them and called out:

"Grandyfellow! What are you doing here? And who's that?"

"You may speak," Stephen whispered, "along the lines we discussed. You may not complain or warn them."

Mr. Grandyfellow smiled, showing all of his little white teeth, and said: "Got another one for the galley!"

"He's a little old, isn't he?" said the fairy who had spoken.

But the other fairy, a darker creature with black hair, was staring intently at Stephen. All of a sudden he broke out:

"He's eaten our food, hasn't he?"

"Many, many years ago," Mr. Grandyfellow said. "He's one that got away."

"Well done Grandy!" the dark fairy exclaimed. "Well done!"

"Thank you," Mr. Grandyfellow said. "I was just putting him to work."

"Are you daft?" the dark fairy said. "Bring him upstairs! The King will want to see him first."

"Very well," Mr. Grandyfellow said, and jerked on the silver chain around Stephen's neck. "Come along, you. Time to meet King Oberon."

For a moment their eyes met, and it was Stephen who smiled, very mildly. Mr. Grandyfellow looked away.

They walked up a dark, tightly spiralling staircase. The music, the feet stomping on the floorboards and the hubble of voices, grew louder and louder. At the top a metal door grinded open and they entered a long corridor.

Cobwebs clung in the cracks and corners of the stone ceiling. The tapestries hanging from the cold walls were stained and tattered, and the carpet was crooked. At the end of the hallway was an enormous wooden door, presided over on either side by enormous marble statues, one of a lion, and the other of a unicorn.

The dark fairy waved his hand, and the doors slowly swung inwards, revealing a spacious ballroom. The music streamed out like water from a dam that had burst. Dancers circled around the room like they were being sucked down a whirlpool. They were very thin, almost emaciated, and their clothes did not fit them well. The grins on their faces were stretched too tight, so that they looked like they were in the extremity of some powerful emotion, or terrible pain, and they were speaking quickly, hysterically, as if they were trying to give the impression of having a very good time.

The head table sat at the far end of the room underneath stag heads mounted on the stone wall. The light coming in through the windows, very high up on the walls, was exceedingly dim, but King Oberon was still clearly visible. He seemed to glow, as pale and distinct as the moon. The courtiers on his either side were as thin and as wretched as the dancers but Oberon was healthy and strong, with shimmering hair and lively green eyes and a silver crown on his head.

"Come with me," Mr. Grandyfellow said, and they made a path through the dancers towards the King.

"Grandyfellow," the voice boomed across the room. "Who is this old man you have brought me?"

The dancers kept madly tilting around them, sometimes leaning almost parallel to the floor, chattering at each other hysterically, their grins painfully carved into their faces. Mr. Grandyfellow and Stephen were not clear of them until they were almost at the table.

And now Stephen got a clear look at the musicians. They were fat little men with thick beards and curly hair, and, in contrast to the suffering dancers, they were playing their pipes, flutes and fiddles without any effort. Stephen looked one of them, a lutist, in the eye, and was startled when the musician's eyes changed from blue to black and then back to blue again.

"Look carefully, your majesty," Mr. Grandyfellow said. "Look very closely."

The king leaned forward across his table. Stephen noted that only the king appeared to be eating. Everyone else's plates bore rotten food that was covered with dirt and cobwebs. The king's plate, on the other hand, was loaded with unusual bones.

"He has eaten my food," the king finally declared, narrowing his eyes. "Look at him. Look at him!"

The king threw up his hands in disgust.

"You've joined this feast years ago," the king said. "Do you know that?"

"Yes, your majesty," Stephen said.

"You accepted my invitation with the very first bite," Oberon continued, his green eyes sparkling like gemstones. "And here you are, late to the party."

The courtiers on Oberon's either side, weak and thin, laughed at this. The music kept blaring from the corner of the room.

"Here I am," Stephen said humbly.

Oberon watched Stephen for a while, a look of astonishment on his face. There was something about this new visitor that he could not quite put his finger on. Something in his bearing. A quality he had that was more alien to the king than any human emotion he had ever beheld in his very, very, very long life. What was it? It was not courage, precisely, though it was very like it. It was instead a kind of quietness where there should be noise. So peculiar!

"Bring him here," Oberon said. "Let him sit at my right hand. The last guest is the dearest, as the saying goes."

Mr. Grandyfellow threw one last imploring glance at Stephen, who shook his head. Oberon saw the gesture and his eyes narrowed.

"What was that?" he said, as Mr. Grandyfellow led Stephen to the king's side. "What was that? Wait. Do I smell iron?"

"I'm sorry my liege," Mr. Grandyfellow howled as he dropped the chain and raised his hands. There was an enormous burst of crackling noise, a terrible smell of ozone, a flash of light, and the music stopped.

Stephen threw a quick, short punch, a right hook, and struck Oberon hard above his left eye with his iron knuckles. Oberon gave a shout and fell backwards, away from the table. Stephen vaulted over the table, knocking the golden plates and the little bones onto the floor, and tried to use the iron chain to bind the king of the fairies.

All of the dancers had collapsed to the floor. They lay with their limbs tangled together like they had been gassed. The only sound they were making now was a strained whooping noise as they struggled to breathe.

"How dare you?" Oberon screamed, his green eyes burning like candles. "How dare you lay your hands on me?"

Something struck Stephen from behind and he was hurled away from the king. It was the dark fairy who had led them to the ballroom, wielding a shillelagh of glowing oak.

"Grandyfellow, help me!" Stephen cried.

Another bolt of light, and the dark fairy was lifted off his feet and sent flying into the pile of musicians.

Stephen tried to get up to his feet, the iron clinking in his hands, but his old bones were too slow. Oberon raised one hand and gestured and both Grandyfellow and the blue fairy (who were wrestling together) vanished. Their clothes dropped to the ground in loose and empty piles, and a moment later, two hares wriggled loose and hopped away.

"You dare come here," Oberon began, "and lay hands on my royal person! I shall ..."

But then Oberon stopped, and cocked his head. A look of understanding filled his glowing, alien eyes.

"My servants!" he cried, and began to run, fleet-footed as the wind, over the fallen bodies of the starving, gasping dancers.

Stephen, heavy with iron, blundered after him. The chain around his neck and in his hands made a heavy clanking noise. His feet came down on the mass of bodies lying on the ground and a few times he came close to stumbling or worse, turning an ankle. But eventually he passed through the great wooden door and raced down the stone hallway to the staircase that led down into the kitchen.

It was deserted, with dirty dishes broken and scattered over the floor, the fires unattended, sloppy grey dishwater pooled in the corners. Not a child was to be seen. And the back door was hanging open, letting the moonlight shine in.

Stephen barged out into the night air, and sprinted around the corner of the castle until he came to the glimmering path of mother of pearl. Oberon was standing there with his hands raised in the air, making a high-pitched, chattering, clicking noise like the mesmerizing call of a predator instinct. And the bodies of the children lay prostrate on the path ahead of him. They had eaten the King's food, and they were under his spell.

And so had Stephen, of course, but the horseshoe was still lying cold and heavy against his heaving chest. The fairy king's song had no effect upon him. Instead, he ploughed into Oberon's back, parallel to the ground, like a blindside-flanker making a flying tackle. Oberon made a completely inhuman noise, and his strange song stopped. The children began to stir.

"Run!" Stephen roared, his voice full of furious command. "Follow the path to the door! And close it after you!"

He could not look up to see if they were listening. Oberon was twisting underneath him, not like a bucking animal so much as like a transforming piece of machinery. The only constant in all the activity was the green eyes, burning and glowing, almost smoking in the mist.

Stephen threw punches with his right hand and used his left to try to entangle the King with the chain. It was no use; Oberon's form was constantly shifting, twisting, and there was nowhere to hook it, nothing on which it would catch.

Finally, Oberon was loose. He did not throw Stephen off, instead, he simply disappeared from beneath him, and appeared to his right in the form of an enormous stag. There was a brief instant, the fragile, ephemeral moment that exists at the heart of every story, where Stephen's adventure trembled on the verge between triumph and tragedy. And in that moment, Stephen quickly looped the end of the iron chain around the stag's hind leg, and fastened it tight.

The stag bounded away, its hindquarters working smoothly and powerfully, as it dragged Stephen along the path by his neck.

Sky and the earth moved in and out, and rapidly alternated places with one another. Jagged bits of shell dug into his cheeks and his forehead, and his aged skeleton was slammed into the ground, again and again, as the stag bounded up and lightly landed. The chain tightened around his neck, so that he was afraid his neck would snap.

Things grew dark and he realized they were in the woods. By how much had he slowed the king? How fast could the little children run? How far was it to the door? He tried to look ahead of him but he couldn't see anything past the hindquarters of the stag.

And then there was the sound of one child screaming, quickly joined by several more. The stag made a satisfied grunting sound and lurched forward with increased urgency. And Stephen, reflecting wearily that no matter how much you worked, the task was never quite done, that there was always just a *little* more required, managed to turn his body around so that he was travelling feet first through the air. When he landed he dug his heels into the ground, and he wrapped both of his hands around the iron chain, and when the stag tried to take another leap he pulled with all his might, so that its forward momentum was halted and it stumbled to its knees, one of its back legs suspended in the air.

Stephen could finally see the children, and they were indeed crowded around the door, climbing up and hopping through one at a time. Jessica was helping them up and staring back at her pursuers with eyes as big as saucers.

The stag let out a keening cry, and it shifted, transformed, with a movement like a candle melting. Its front legs stretched out like arms so that it began to look like a hybrid, a centaur. Its head becoming the head of a man.

Stephen hauled back on the chain until suddenly he toppled over onto his back. The chain had come loose. And the monster galloped on all fours towards the children like a gorilla running on is knuckles, snorting and panting and growling. But it was too late. The last child hopped up through the door and Jessica followed. She looked at Stephen for one brief moment, her eyes shining with tears, and then she slammed the door shut.

The King of the Fairies howled.

Stephen, for his part, worked to loosen the chain around his neck. The world was going grey, very grey, and the pain was so acute he could barely think. His fingers fumbled numbly at the links but they couldn't get in. His chest started hitching, jerking, like a broken machine that wouldn't switch off. Finally the pain disappeared, turning into a milky, relaxed feeling, and his hands fell at his sides. He knew he was going to die. And just then, something began to whisper at his neck, and he felt the chain come undone and land on the path beside his head. He took a great, whooping breath of air and sat up with his hands at his neck. Out of the corner of his eye he saw the green vines that had unwrapped the chains sliding back into the forest. And then he became conscious of Oberon looming over him, the heavy sound of his breathing, and he remembered Grandyfellow's warnings. So he let go of his neck, cleared his throat as best he could, and lifted his gaze to meet his fate.

It had taken many years, and much uncharacteristic discipline, for the fairies to convince mankind that they did not exist. And so, there was some understandable trepidation after the escape. The sudden appearance of twenty seven children, most of them speaking dialects (or even languages) that had not been spoken in England for many, many years, might be expected to provoke a great deal of human curiosity, or even hostility. The fairies had not closely watched humanity for some time, but what they knew disturbed them a great deal. They had no idea whether humans, with the new wizardry called science, might be able to break into the fairy world, and what kind of damage they might be able to inflict upon doing so.

What a relief then, that humanity preferred any explanation to the obvious one. The fairies returned to their dancing and feasts, joking about the stupidity of the humans, their thick-headedness, their lack of intellectual dexterity, promising to play tricks on them on the future. But all of them, secretly, rather relieved.

Of course Jessica was grateful to have escaped, but she could not help worrying of poor Stephen, who had given so much to save them all. Her mind kept returning to the site of him sitting on that pale white path, his face brick red and starved for oxygen, before she slammed the door. Was he dead? And if not, what horrible fate had the fairies inflicted upon him?

Perhaps a fairy could sense her distress, and took pity on her (for no fairy is wholly evil, just as they are never wholly good) because not long after returning to Canada she had an unusual dream. She saw Oberon drag Stephen back to his court. The King bound Stephen's hands with golden chains and then hurled invective at him from upon his throne, while the fairies and the dancers and the musicians crowded around him, leering and jabbing him with sticks.

But no matter how they tried, they could not disturb Stephen's equilibrium. He regarded them steadily, calmly, answering their questions and picking himself up carefully after every blow. Eventually it became a sport with the fairies, to try to startle Stephen, to upset him, to make loud noises or to transform themselves into unusual forms, in an attempt to force him into a reaction. But as Stephen steadfastly regarded all of their tricks without any emotion, they grew more and more delighted at his reactions (or, more precisely, of his lack of any reaction at all). The king had never before met a man like Stephen, and he was endlessly fascinated by him.

It was not long, of course, before the dance resumed (with Grandyfellow cleaning dishes, alone, down in the galley). The musicians took up their instruments, the dancers resumed their pirouettes, and Oberon the Great and Terrible took his place at the head table and began his joyful feast. But now, something was different.

Stephen, unchained, moved among the dancers with a tray of silver cups. His tread was confident and firm and the dancers parted for him like a school of fish around a pillar of coral. In all that hysteria, the laughter and weeping, the exhaustion and pain, he was an oasis of stoicism. Like a cool breeze. Everyone who met his eye, as they circled round and round that room, forever, saw a will that would never break. A slight nod of his head was all it took to restore flagging spirits. Because dignity comes not from courage strength but pain and weakness. It is noble delusion set up as a shield against the howling insanity of this world, and every other, as fragile as dream, as enduring as hope, as contagious as a cold. Even there, in that grey eternal sunset, in that silent world, in the light of that cold and distant moon.

About the Author

Cliff Jackman first captured international attention with the 2010 release of his first book, ***Deeper,*** a critically acclaimed collection of intriguing short stories that had critics favourably comparing him to Stephen King. Jackman followed this success with the release of his widely praised debut novel, ***The Black Box***, in 2012 and has now returned to the world of short stories in 2013 with what is perhaps his finest work to date: ***Jackman's Cliff***. Jackman was born in Deep River and raised in Ottawa. He received a Bachelor's in English from York University, a Master's in English from Queen's University, and a Bachelor of Laws from Osgoode Hall Law School. The writer and practicing lawyer lives in Guelph and works in Toronto where he finds no end of inspiration for the colourful characters that populate his books.

Manor House Publishing
www.manor-house.biz
905-648-2193